DANCE
OF THE
FATHERS
And Other Stories

DANCE OF THE FATHERS
And Other Stories

Nemen M. Kpahn

Village Tales Publishing

MINNEAPOLIS, MN

A catalog record for this book is available from the Library of Congress:
Library of Congress Control Number: 2023905354
ISBN: 9781945408960
eISBN: 9781945408977

Published By:
Village Tales Publishing
Minneapolis, MN 55429

Layout and Cover Design by: OASS
www.villagetales.com
www.villagetalespublishing.com

Dedication

This collection is dedicated to my mother,
Martha Kwalea Bahn Kpahn,
who allowed me, as a child, to read
as much as I wanted.

Also by Nemen M. Kpahn

Drama on Pipe Line Road
Little Brave Lydia
A Naked Lie: and other stories
The Fading Flower

Contents

Preface

The Liberian civil was a watershed moment in West African history. For a long time after 1960, West Africa was a sub-region prone to coups, while East Africa was a sub-region known for civil and guerrilla wars. However, the narrative changed in late 1989 when Charles Taylor and a group of marauding rebels invaded Liberia from the Ivory Coast to overthrow the despotic regime of President Samuel K. Doe. As Elizabeth Blunt, the famous former BBC West Africa correspondent, recalled, the Liberian civil war was sad and brutal. It was a tragic story of mostly men and young boys with guns unleashing barbarity on their compatriots. But even amid such brutality in Liberia, there were still moments of fun and hilarity. Unfortunately, very few stories are written about what life was like behind rebel lines in the 1990s in Liberia; the stories are predominantly based on first-hand accounts of things that happened to ordinary people during traumatic times. I consider myself a troubadour and a storyteller. My job is to ensure that the difficulties ordinary people experience are never forgotten. Future generations must constantly be reminded of those dark days, never to repeat them. That is why I wrote these collections of stories, which I hope you will enjoy.

I am immensely grateful to Ms. Ophelia S. Lewis, a gem of a publisher and consultant.

*Friendship is a beautiful thing that can bring
people from different walks of life and backgrounds
uniquely together. My friend and I story is about two
boyhood friends, Dahn, a bright and erudite boy, and
Woto, a worldly-wise hustler, who become best bud-
dies. One day Woto disappears, and Dahn goes on to
become a high school principal. Years later, during the
war, the two friends reunited astonishingly with even
more surprising and unexpected results.*

My friend and I

Even though the voice on the radio is far away in
London, most Liberians seemed to recognize it. A man
on the BBC African Service flagship program, *Focus on
Africa*, was claiming he had launched a rebel group to
overthrow President Samuel K. Doe. Everyone knew
the President had rigged the 1985 Presidential elections and prolonged his stay in power protected by
his elite Israeli trained Special Anti-Terrorist Unit
(SATU). As long as the President had the loyalty of

these men with guns, his grip on power was secured. This feared SATU Presidential guard battalion members were mainly drawn from President Doe's ethnic group and were fiercely loyal to him. There was no way the entrenched President could leave power through the force of arms except in his own time and choosing.

It was December 1989; the festive season of Christmas had everyone in a holiday mood. December weather in the highland region of this northeastern county of Liberia was cool, with a dewy haze brought upon by the advent of the cool Harmattan winds that blew southwards from the Sahara to the north. The rice harvest was in the barns, and farmers dependent on shifting cultivation methods had not yet selected new sites for next year's farming. This was a time of peace and happiness. Family members visited each other to swap tales of the ancestors, romance, and great heroes of the tribe and county. People were incredibly generous with food and their time during this festive season.

In the olden days, new songs and plays sprang out of nowhere and became national anthems in the towns and villages surrounding Tappeta in Lower Nimba County. From Graie to Toweh Town, Ziah to Vahn Town, and Diallah. Now though, everyone knew technology was displacing the old ways. Young people carried battery-powered cassette tape recorders on their shoulders, playing the latest Harry Konah and Kennedy Wogbeh songs.

The young men were resting and enjoying the break from labor between the harvest and the next farming seasons, taking leisurely strolls during the evening hours in Banligeah, Granpea, and other towns and villages. As was the fashion, cheap colorful towels draped around their necks. To get the attention of the young women, they adorn themselves in muscle T-shirts displaying bulging biceps.

To the surprise and chagrin of many, the announcement on BBC turned out to be the sad truth that Charles Taylor's rebel army calling themselves the National Patriotic Front of Liberia, had succeeded in driving out the civil administration and the much-hated Armed Forces of Liberia (AFL) from Nimba County. The AFL, in theory, was the national army of Liberia; but in practice, sometimes functioned as an ethnic militia carrying out atrocities against the civilian population in this hotbed of anti-government sentiments and rebellion called Nimba County.

From its inception, this war of attrition pitched a ruthless American-trained army against a brutal rebel force. Young and inexperienced rebel fighters with expert local knowledge defeated the government army and put in place a ragtag administration with rebel generals and commanders serving as legislators and administrators all at the same time.

General Woto, a colorful character of unpredictable ways, became one of the county's new strongmen. These new defacto rulers played the role of both civilian and security personnel in the county, replacing all forms of the old governmental civil representation.

Woto, within a short period, rose from obscurity to become a rebel general. Folks said Woto hailed from a family of indentured laborers working the fields of wealthy men like Paramount Chief Gongbay before the war. Everyone knew Woto to be a car loader at the main parking station in Tappeta, always looking unkempt, aggressive, and honey-tongued at the same time. Woto did not like the menial labor of farming and the drudgery of farm work his parents performed, so he left Gbanipea a few miles west of Tappeta and settled here. After the failed 1985 coup of the late General Quiwonkpa and the ugly reprisals undertaken against the people of Nimba, Woto disappeared from the central parking of Tappeta. The women who prepared GB and sold them in the lappa bi-door (food kiosks where cloths served as doors) cook shops missed him along with those who operated opium dens commonly called *ghetto*, which he frequented after work.

Some said Woto drifted to the artisanal goldmines of Rivercess County. Others said he migrated to Voinjama doing what he did best, loading passenger cars with people and goods for a fee. Still, others said Woto followed a Vai woman and settled along the shore of Lake Piso, selling fish caught along the shores of the mysterious lake to tourists.

Whatever happened, people in Lower Nimba stopped seeing Woto out of the blue. However, for the good people of the district, there were children to feed and send to school and houses to be built. Young men and women, and even older people, had to marry and get engaged. Life was like that, *gbesuluku*; someday good, someday bad. And soon, Woto, the flamboyant car loader, was forgotten except by his poor mother, who was also clueless about what happened to her son. Apart from his mother, Pillar, one person who did not also forget Woto and kept wondering what happened to his friend was Dahn.

Dahn, a shy but bookish young man, often wondered where his childhood friend was. Woto and Dahn were the case of opposite attracts. While Woto was flamboyant, aggressive, and irreverent to society and humanity, Dahn was ambitious and wanted to be successful. Education offered Dahn that opportunity. He attended the University of Liberia on a government scholarship majoring in Education, and returned to Tapeta a few years later to become principal of Tappeh Memorial High School, the premier public high school in the district. To the surprise of many, Woto and Dahn kept the ties that bind them strongly together after Dahn's return to Tappeta. While Woto loaded cars and drank profusely, Dahn supervised more than 1000 students and 50 teachers in the public high school.

Before going to college, Dahn shared the same room and did everything with Woto. Both young men loved cooking dry rice. This simple meal was always cooked at night after spending the entire day hustling to get the ingredients and then cooking and eating late at night. In the evening, when Woto came home late after hustling at the parking, he brought sardines and pepper. Dahn, an enterprising cook, would convert the meagre ingredients into a sumptuous meal of sardine mixed in red oil and pepper, adding a little bit of salt and Maggie cubes to the rice.

Dahn's poor old parents lived in Zuolay, waiting for the day God would call them home. He completed Zuolay Public School, which ended in the 9th Grade, and then had to move further south to live in Tappeta, the district headquarters, to complete his high school at the same school he was now Principal of. Dahn knew the pain of being snubbed by girls and looked down upon because of his impoverished and deprived background. Woto also knew the pain of rejection because of his background, but he turned the pain into street smartness, mastering the ability to survive and make money.

It was almost a comical sight years later in Tappeta to see the bookish Dahn dressed in a white ironed monogram shirt and the irreverent Woto dressed in faded T-shirts and jeans. Together, the two young men would head to the palm wine station near the wine booths a few meters away from the small Jehovah's Witness Kingdom Hall near Gwen Creek in Central Tappeta. The atmosphere in the rickety palm wine booths of makeshift corrugated iron sheets and bare wooden benches for seats was always exuberant as the winebibbers drank the cool sappy white natural palm wine. Their bushy moustaches often sifted the wine from the insects and bugs who, like their human counterparts, shared an affinity for this mildly alcoholic drink. The palm wine was sold out of big 5-gallon wine containers in plastic cups of varying sizes, depending on the amount paid by young women.

Dahn often wondered about Woto after his friend disappeared without a trace. Then one day, when rebel fighters swept down south from the hills of the north, a new phase of life began. There was no more school for Dahn to be the principal of. There were no teachers or students to supervise. His carefully cultivated middle-class life disappeared. There were no more regular shops to buy provisions from. No more salary and no money to cater to his family. His status as a community leader dissipated. Now it was these rebel generals called COs, a short name for Commanding Officers, who controlled everything. Money, power, and, most importantly, guns. Those who wielded them became unquestioned leaders of the land.

Reduced to penury, Dahn had to make a choice, either join the rebel insurgents in their fight against President Samuel Doe and contend with the jealousies, infighting, and resentment among rebel ranks against intellectuals and anyone perceived as being part of the elites. Or wait for a return to normalcy when schools will re-open for him to become Primo (Principal) again.

While in principle, Dahn supported the rebel goal of forcefully removing President Samuel Doe from power, the prospect of killing another human being filled him with trepidation. Rebel fighters' wanton cruelty to civilians, their mercurial tempers, and their callous disregard for human life made him want to stay quiet and lay low. Sometimes fate can be unnecessarily cruel. So, by default, Dahn chose the latter course of action, waiting for the war to end.

But children's mouths, crying to be fed, could not wait for the war to end. His wife also needed deodorant and other things. He needed things like batteries for his transistor radio and shavers. There were no shops open. All the stores and shops in Tappeta had been looted and vandalized by rebel fighters and their civilian collaborators. Markets, apart from those that sold foodstuffs, were non-existent. The road to the capital that brought supplies to Tappeta had been cut off, and no supplies came in.

Desperation to meet the needs of himself and his family drove Dahn to leave his cocoon existence of penury. There had been talks that if one managed to cross the border into the Ivory Coast, one could contact friends and relatives abroad who could send some money through Western Union to buy food and supplies. Dahn had never left the borders of Liberia before. He thought of going to contact his nephew and some of his former students who now called the US home. Dahn kept putting the decision off, and the need got greater until finally, Weamie, one of his former students, offered to accompany him to Danane, Ivory Coast.

Unfortunately, public transport has become non-existent. The Mandingo people, geniuses at servicing, managing, and controlling anything that moved, fearing rebel advances, had fled north into Guinea.

Further complicating everything, rebel soldiers and generals commandeered everything that moved and some static ones, such as beautiful houses, machines, women, and men, for themselves in their war of liberation.

General Woto, the feared rebel general, had returned to Lower Nimba as a hero. What other status is a man required to succeed in life? Woto had earned the highest accolade available in rebel territory. He was a Special Forces Commando trained in Burkina Faso and Libya and was head of the NPFL Cobra Battalion with a reputation for fearlessness and wanton cruelty.

One Saturday afternoon, when Woto visited Graie, the women of the township put their lappas on the ground for Woto to walk on. This township serves as a crossroad, connecting Tappeta to Saclepea and Ganta to the north and Toweh Town to the east, and, crucially, connecting to the Ivory Coast. In his right hand, Woto carried a cow tail adorned with cowrie shells, the ultimate symbol of power and authority. A band of bodyguards accompanied him, occasionally shooting bursts of staccato Ak-47-gun shots into the air, much to the amusement and excitement of the singing and dancing crowd eulogizing him. Woto, now and then, would pause and throw money into the air, and people would scramble and fight over them as they fell to the ground. His car, a captured late model Nissan Patrol, carried two human skulls tied to the two side mirrors. Woto enjoyed the adulation, power, and attention basking in it, all smiling from ear to ear and waving broadly, basking in the attention. Who could imagine a son of indentured laborers and drifters being one of the most powerful men in Liberia? Life can change!

Not far from Graie, from the direction of the south, two men walked towards the town. From the direction of Zuolay southward to Tappeta, Dahn mopped the sweat across his brows. His legs ached, and he was tired. He wanted to sit somewhere to rest, but his young companion, Weamie, was having none of it.

"Sir, the journey is still far. We must reach Zuatuo at least before we can rest and sleep. We still have Toweh Town, Sarlay, Beatuo, and the entire Niquea territory to pass. We cannot afford to rest now, Sir."

Dahn nodded his head. Twenty kilometers of walking sapped the energy out of him, but he needed to push on. His legs felt like lead under him, but he could not stop.

Ahead of them, the sounds of drumming, singing, and festivities drifted. The exhilarating sounds of drumbeats, music, dust, and joy of festivities made the two travelers hasten their steps. The endless trail of rebel checkpoints dotting every town and village along the main road from Yreah Town all the way here had taken its toll on the men walking.

At each of these rebel checkpoints, travelers were either welcome to a friendly chat and gossip or harassment or extortion. Usually, though, a mixture of friendliness and extortion is applied in equal measures. Exerting superhuman efforts, Dahn and Weamie hastened on foot to Graie.

On the outskirts of the sizable town, the two men met a 10-year-old boy hunting birds with his sling slot. He was one of those kids who seemed to know everything about the town and everyone.

"Pekin, what's happening in the town?" Dahn called out to the kid.

"Ah papay, you don't know? The great General Woto, the man who, when Doe soldiers hear his name, they run, is in town with his men. They are sleeping in town tonight, and everybody is happy. My sister Ophelia and everybody, including the chiefs, is with him."

"Wow! Thank you, my Pekin. I wonder which Woto the kid is talking about," Dahn asked loudly.

"Sir, it is Woto who once upon a time was loading cars for a fee. Didn't I hear you and him were best of friends?"

"What do you mean? In general, people are talking about my childhood friend, Woto Gongbay?

"Certainly Sir."

"Weamie, I am so happy that my man, my long-time best friend, Woto, is in town. Oh, God can bless people at strange times. I can't believe Woto is alive and such a big man. We must go and see him! God, thank you for Woto oh," Dahn gesticulated lifting his hands to God above in praises. "I know my time has come. The way I've been suffering for so long, the moment I talk to my friend, he will help me with something."

"Sir, I would humbly suggest we leave Woto alone and continue our journey," Weamie suggested. "People can change. Power corrupts and corrupts absolutely. The Woto you knew way back may not be the same Woto who is a general today."

"Boy, how dare you," Dahn said. "Do you know that Woto, and I shared everything together? Do you know Woto, and I are a band of brothers? We lived in the same room, cooked together, ate together, cried together, danced together, and played together."

When Weamie did not respond, Dahn said, "I will forgive you for your statement because you are too young to understand the kind of friendship that existed between Woto and I. Our friendship those days were strong and thick, not the fickle things you young men today call friendship. Follow me and see."

Dahn turned to the young boy and said, "Pekin, which part of town is Woto?"

Pointing in the direction of the town's palaver hut, the boy said, "Just go straight to that intersection, then turn left towards Chief Wonnah Wehyee's house, C.O. Woto is there. You will see the people dancing from afar."

Weamie started to say something, but the look on his senior companion's face silenced him. He meekly followed, although with reservation. He adopted Dahn's brisk strides. The frenzied sound of drumbeats and excited voices grew louder as they got closer.

When they got there, overcome with joy, Dahn pushed his way through the crowd elbowing people left and right to get out of his way. Many looked at him with disbelief. Dahn made it through to the point where he could see his friend. Woto's bushy beard now had strains of grey in it, and his girth had grown wider, but the General had not changed much in the nearly ten years Dahn had not seen him.

"Oh, thank God to see you, my friend," Dahn shouted, walking toward Woto.

A team of bodyguards comprised of armed teenagers ran to block Dahn's path. Woto immediately recognized Dahn.

"Oh, my friend, it has been so long," he shouted. "I'm so glad to see you!"

Woto's overzealous bodyguards immediately recoiled.

"The pleasure is mine," Dahn said.

The two men embraced with warm affection. They held each tightly for a minute. They had so much to catch up on. Life can change, so it had!

"Hey, bring a bottle of beer for my good friend," Woto ordered.

From behind Woto's highchair, what looked like a bottle of expensive champagne surfaced and was thrust into Dahn's hands. Dahn had not laid eyes on a bottle of cold beer for a long time since the rebels' occupation.

"Bring food and more drinks for my friend," Woto demanded.

The sight and aroma of the food were a gentle massage to Dahn's soul. Famished, he ate the food like a child who hadn't seen food for weeks. He sank his teeth into the flesh of a chicken thigh and winked at his young companion, who also seemed to enjoy sipping the cold beer in his hand.

Dahn's third bottle of cold Club beer had barely touched his lips when the wild sound of a command cut through the celebration.

"Commandos!"

Everyone froze.

"Brave, strong . . . intelligent!"

The crowd of mostly young men and a few female rebel soldiers responded in unison, forming a line, holding their Kalashnikov rifles and rocket propelled grenade launcher tubes above their heads.

"How's the CO?"

"Alright . . . Alright . . . Alright!" the rebel soldiers broke into a rapturous song.

General Woto loved the praises of his men and women fighters.

"Soldier!" General Woto shouted, not mentioning anyone's name.

A short heavy set muscular rebel soldier stepped forward.

"Rebel Jacket, flog this man 25 lashes!"

Instantly, the heavy-set man grabbed Dahn and dragged him from his chair. Then several pairs of rough hands held his legs, hands, and head. Reality sank in. How could he be sipping beer and joking one minute, and the next, he was lying across a dirty floor on his stomach with his bottom up?

The pain took over a portion of Dahn's brain as the rattan cane tore into his rear end.

"Woto, it is me," Dahn shouted at the top of his lungs. "What have I done to deserve this beating?"

"Of course, Dahn, it is you," Woto responded. "I know it is you."

The soldier waited for Woto's next order.

"Who told you to stop?" Woto shouted at the soldier.

Then the whip descended and ascended in the rhythmic motion of searing pain tearing through Dahn's body.

Woto nodded at the soldier and shouted, "As you were, Soldier!"

The beating stopped!

A bemused sadistic smile covered Woto's face.

Two soldiers pulled Dahn to his feet and carried him back to his seat beside General Woto's chair.

"Why Woto?" Dahn asked, his voice filled with hurt, bewilderment, and contempt. "Why?"

Woto's brain came fully alive; it flashed an electric smirk. Anyone smirking with such electric glee has stories to tell.

"Dahn, we did everything together," Woto said. "When we were young, I would go on the hustle just to make sure there was food for you to eat when you got home. We shared the same clothes and even dated the same girls. I was making an investment in you. But as you can see, education does not matter anymore; it is gun that matters. I wanted to show you that now, I have power, and I can do anything I want. Even now, if I kill you, nothing will happen to me. But of course, I will not kill you because you are my friend."

Dahn sighed.

"Soldiers!" Woto shouted. "Bring more beer for this man. Give him two bags of rice for his family and a box of fish."

Two hundred-pound bags of parboiled rice and a case of frozen casava fish were brought and set before Dahn.

"Where were you headed to, Dahn?" Woto asked.

"Ivory Coast," Dahn mumbled.

"Well, good friend, my jeep will take you to the border," Woto offered.

"I'm okay, General Woto," Dahn replied. "You have done enough for me today. I will get there on my own way."

"Nonsense," Woto said. "My car will take you straight to the border while my men take the rice and fish to your family in Tappeta"

Woto's men release a volley of shots into the air while shouting, "Tie-bay he-ah! Tie-bay he-ah!"

The rebel soldiers were anxious for blood. Mischief kept them feeling more alive. It was part of the way they live and play. Tie bay was a form of punishment where one's hands were pulled towards your back and tied together, raising it high beyond tolerance.

Dahn caught Weamie's eyes and read deep concern. He hoped Dahn would accept the General's kindness and do so quickly. The sooner they leave, the better off they would be.

Dahn's buttocks were struggling to recover from the beating he'd received. There is damage to the skin, but the damage to the brain will take far longer to heal. Yet, he was grateful to be traveling in a car instead of walking.

Weamie saw the pain written across Dahn's face and wryly said, "Sir, we should have continued our journey without stopping in Graie to greet your friend."

"I think so, too," Dahn replied.

They were both happy that Ivory Coast inched closer.

A young woman, her young children, a dead husband, bloodthirsty rebels, and prison all add to an intriguing story based partly on an actual incident that occurred behind rebel lines in 1990 wartime Liberia.

She will live

In this part of Liberia was extremely difficult to know; whether one was in Liberia or Sierra Leone. Although the two countries were neighbors, small, and both English-speaking, no two neighbors' accents could be so different. Here in this part of Liberia, nestled close to the Sierra Leonian border at the foothills of the famous Kangbo Hills, farmers tended to their rice crops and harvested sorghum in this fertile valley. Monrovia lay southwards, while Voinjama, the county headquarter was northward and the border town of Bomaru in Sierra Leone was less than 10 kilometers away. Most people here went to school in Sierra Leone and the local Mande language was spoken in both countries. The kinship ties among the people surpassed the artificial border divides imposed by the white man during colonialism.

Life, slow, predictable, hard, and cozy in varying degrees, continued for the conservative and hardy inhabitants until the marauders arrived, driving away the small detachment of government soldiers into Sierra Leone without a fight. Soon fighters from other parts of Liberia brought a mixture of excitement, especially for the youths with their colorful nom de guerre, classy jeans, wigs, and an assortment of weapons.

Among the fighters was Rebel Madame. A tough wiry young woman in her early twenties with short, cropped hair and tattooed arms notorious for her penchant for brutality. An engaging character oozing charisma, Rebel Madame was loathed, feared, loved, and hated in equal measure. A character that evoked strong feelings, she cared less for what people thought of her. She always wore an impervious amulet said to protect her from the enemy's bullet on her forearm. Rebel Madame's other trademark was her fondness for blue jeans pants and round-neck T-shirts, never a collared one. While other rebel fighters could be seen walking in the town occasionally without their rifles, Rebel Madame was never seen without her automatic rifle. Rumour has it that even when making love, her loaded rifle was right under her head.

Rebel Madame was one of the few female rebel fighters residents in Vahun. People wondered why Rebel Madame was so tough. Her voice, while shrill, carried a forceful tone and when Rebel Madame wanted to sing and dance, the entire Vahun jumped for joy, hearing a such melodious voice. There was something about her upbringing that put her on edge.

A few years, at the start of the Liberian civil war, Kou, before she became Rebel Madame, was a gifted and quiet schoolgirl who dreamed of becoming a nurse. Then one day when government soldiers who said they were chasing rebels ransacked her village, burned their house, and killed her parents in a way too gruesome to describe here. Kou hid in the coffee bush near her house, watching her parents' house burnt, and heard the pitiful cries of her parents pleading for mercy, a plead ultimately unsuccessful as life was snuffed out of them. From that moment on rage, terrible and dark took over Kou. She did not care for the wider politics or exergies of the war. All Kou wanted was revenge, a burning desire to inflict pain on members of the Armed Forces of Liberia by killing them and leaving their families and children orphans like she was.

From her training days in the tough camp at Gborplay to the battles in Ganta, Pallala, and other towns, Kou had become a gripe lip killer and battle-hardened fighter respected and feared by her male colleagues. Her posting to the sleepy town of Vahun was more of a recuperating ground for her as she suffered shrapnel wounds to her stomach during fierce skirmishes with soldiers in the fight to take over Voinjama.

While traditionally a sleepy laid-back town, the war has transformed Vahun into a crossroads. Urban dwellers who hailed from Lofa County wanting respite and food away from the internecine war of attrition between rebel warlords fighting in Monrovia and the rubber plantations around the capital made their way to other parts of Lofa through Vahun. Civilians not wanting to be caught in the crossfire of raging bullets and want to avoid the dangers of the main road from Monrovia-Bo Waterside Highway transited here as well. People from Tubmanburg and the mining camps rich in alluvial diamonds, seeking the safety of Sierra Leone, use Vahun as a crossing point to enter Bomaru and move on to Freetown before the country's own civil war.

Twice a week, a convoy arrives to bring war-weary people, usually hungry and penniless, ferried through the courtesy of an operational logging camp at ULC. Some made their way on foot in small groups and by the time they arrived in Vahun the emaciated bodies and sores testified to their ordeals. It was not these small groups arriving in Vahun that the townsfolks and rebel fighters look forward to with some excitement. It was the convoys of men and women, usually of people under forty, that brought life to this town, taking away the mundane mediocrity of existence.

Not only did these people come with hunger and sometimes diseases, but they also brought things like shoes, sneakers, clothes, and whatever they possess. The displaced people, as they were known, or internally displaced peoples or IDPs as humanitarian organizations, preferred to call them, were more often willing to part with what little they still had, after crossing the gauntlet of checkpoints from Monrovia for little food, a warm bed, and a bath. What excited the rebel fighters and the youths of the town the most, was the prospect of getting sexual partners. Gone were the days when a man wanted a woman to propose love to her; the woman would say let me go and tell my mom or aunty your proposal. There was no longer let us study each other's ways for six months and let's see if we are compatible. In a land of war and hunger, the new slogan was 'make it quick.'

So, as soon as fighters heard the blaring of horns, they all rushed to the S2 or military intelligence office. This cluster of modern office buildings used to be the old produce marketing office head's office in the district converted into office blocks while the back of the warehouse served as a jail for prisoners.

Now the two S2 officers were busy straining the IDPs. There were six rebel fighters guarding the IDPs and they quickly turn over the truckload of civilians soon encircled by fighters and curious youths from Vahun. Everyone's name, previous place of residence, occupation, and destination of travel were lodged into a big folder. Then their belongings were searched for contraband, which in this case meant anything the fighters desired. Either those items were outrightly confiscated or paid for at rock-bottom prices. The few men among this group came in for special scrutiny.

One slim woman in her mid-thirties was especially worried about this screening. In almost all the checkpoints from Bomi Hills here, the rebel fighters were primarily interested in taking their belongings and not where the hell they were going. Now the fighters were recording everything. Her heart missed a beat when their time came for screening. She and her husband hid a deep secret and the end to cross into Sierra Leone was so near and yet so far away.

Then Rebel Madame did what made the woman in her mid-thirties heart missed a beat, nearly collapsing; except for her young son and daughter holding her hands. She needed to be strong for them even when the world around her was imploding. Rebel Madame's frisking hands went around the upper part of her husband's foot, just below the knee, and her shrill voice rang out excitement with bloodlust.

"There is a soldier! Damn, soldier, your own finished today!"

The other rebel fighters loitering around, apparently disinterested, sprang to life breaking into a song. Their rifles held mid-air above their heads, they soon form a circle around the man screaming, yelling, dancing, and shouting staccato bursts of semiautomatic fire into the air as bewildered and terrified civilians looked on.

"This dog meat thinks he's smart. I book him," Rebel Madame shouted. "I felt the boots mark on his foot."

The more experienced displaced people knew then why the fighters were excited. It was a common belief that since government soldiers frequently wore black boots under their uniforms, the boots left a permanent mark on the upper part of the boots. That was why the fighters picked the man up.

And rebel justice was swift. The man was taken away from the cue and escorted away from his crying wife and kids. There was a volley of gunshots, and then it became quiet and noisy again. The fighters were singing and writhing in unexplainable joy. Their killer lust filled the fighters rejoiced.

Rebel Madame pointed her Kalashnikov rifle at the young woman silently weeping with her terrified kids, and said, "Come here! I feel like shooting you. What is your name?"

The woman stared blankly into the skies. The words could not come out of her mouth. Rebel Madame released a volley of shots at close range between the woman's legs and then somehow, she found her voice.

"Ivy," she answered.

"Ivory," Rebel Madame asked. "What kinda stupid name is that?"

The woman said nothing.

"You married a soldier, our enemy, and my enemy. When your husband and his friends invaded my home in Nimba county, they burnt women and children alive in their homes. They robbed me of my mom, brothers, and sisters, leaving me alone in the world. I won't let you suffer that," Rebel Madame said.

The woman listened quietly.

"I, Rebel Madame, will make sure, you, your husband, and these brats of yours will go and grow your family together in the next world."

The devil took hold of the woman at that moment, and she moved quickly. Rebel Mama pressed the trigger. Within the twinkling of an eye, Guva, one of her colleagues, hit the barrel of the rifle, and the bullets hit the ground, narrowly missing Ivy.

"Enough, Rebel Madame," Guva said. "One death for the day is enough."

Her colleagues disarmed her, taking Rebel Madame's rifle away as she screamed obscenities. So extreme was her anger, and so volatile was her temper.

Then the displaced persons now processed, needed to be lodged and there was a rush for the young women, and to a much lesser extent, the young men were offered lodging by generous hosts. Only the older folks in the lodging committee of Vahun had to find empty rooms for themselves in an abandoned warehouse. It was said years later that Rebel Love, a young female fighter, found a husband to father her three children, from among the group of emaciated young men who presented that evening.

That is how Ivy, a high-born young woman of West Indian and Vai heritage, found herself locked up in a small, virtually windowless room somewhere in the jungles of Lofa County in north-western Liberia. The prison was small and hot, with a high roof and a small opening that served as a window. A tiny flicker of sun rays was what made her realize whether it was night or day. Occasionally she heard snippets of conversations and movements of people walking and doing things. She had not had the chance to mourn the demise of her love. The kids, four and six years, cried often asking for their dad or alternatively crying for food. The food consisted of cooked rice sprinkled with a morsel of rotten fish or a piece of vegetable served in the afternoon. The thin mattress on the floor looked more like a straw. She was married to a soldier, but what did she and her kids do to deserve this? Singing and telling stories to the children kept her from growing mad. A heaviness descended on her, and when she tried to think, her mind went blank. She would stare in stupefied silence at the wall. The hours turned to days and then weeks. Nothing, no freedom, no summary kangaroo trial, or execution, just silence.

Gradually, Ivy knew that their lives would be spared because if they wanted to harm them, she and her kids, it would have happened earlier.

Now, something seems to be amiss. The afternoon hours were unusually quiet. The boisterous noises of her minders and their friends suddenly went quiet— no loud vulgar voices, no laughter. Just stillness and the occasional sounds of birds. What was going on? The quietness continued, and then by the time darkness began to descend, and the sounds of mosquitoes flapping their wings returned to the cubicle, activities, loud and irreverent, resumed. Excited voices soon followed by songs.

"The soldier woman and her rats will die oh. . . they will done in their own stew!"

The loud singing brought brutal realities, atrocious and bombastic, to Ivy's ears. Ebenezer and Willete burst out wailing.

"Mama, what is happening," they asked. "Are they going to kill us?"

"No, baby," Ivy said. "They are not going to kill us. Women and children, especially children innocent like you and Willette, are not killed in the war."

"But Mama, listen to what they are saying in the song about us dying," Ebenezer persisted.

"Ebenezer, the fighters often love singing, and there is nothing different today about their singing. Just be quiet before you frighten your little sister."

The singing and hollering drew closer to the prison cell. Ivy held her children closer, crouching over them like a hen protecting her chicks from hawks.

"Mama!" Ebenezer screamed. "They are coming for us to kill us just like they did to daddy!"

"Hey, young man, o ye of little faith. Have you heard what the good Lord did when Daniel was thrown into the lion's den," Ivy reminded. "God sent his angels to close the mouths of the lions, and Daniel was not eaten. Whatsoever happens, our God will protect us."

"God did not protect Papa," he said. "God let those evil men outside take Papa away and shoot him."

Ivy was beside herself in exasperation. Why does this intelligent and bright young child always try to bore holes through her comfort zone? This child did not know that beneath her words of comfort, she was terrified and was only being braved for their sake.

"Ebenezer," she said, "the Lord God moves in mysterious ways. Not because he let those bad men take your father away means he will let them take us away. Give me your hands," she said, "and let us bow our heads and pray. The Lord is a strong tower, the righteous run to Him, and they are saved."

Ivy held her children's hands and started to pray, "Dear Lord . . . ."

The singing and howling outside grew stronger, then objects began hitting their cubicle war. *The soldier woman and her rats will die today!* They sang.

Rebel Madame was getting drunk, doing everything to make herself drunk, but from the look of things, was not having much success, even as she drank the fiery and potent locally distilled gin. She remained lucid as she belched out that the soldier woman will die today!

Rebel Madame gulped an entire bottle of gin down her throat and remained sober. She purposely tried to recollect and regurgitate the images of her parents and siblings burning, but it brought no anger or desire for revenge.

The decision had already been made. Tonight, Ivy and her kids would disappear into eternity. Although she has been comfortable today with the words killed, she could not bring herself to say that word. So, Rebel Madame told herself that the prisoners will disappear. The decision has been made. The lax previous NPFL commander has been replaced by a heartless man determined to write his name in blood in the annals of Vahun's history as a brutish commander. And it was his decision that feeding prisoners were an expensive luxury he could do without. Freeing an innocent woman and her children did not cross his mind.

The decision has been made to make Ivy and her children disappear when darkness came, and most of the good people of Vahun town had gone to sleep; all prisoners would be taken to the dusty road to Sierra Leone and made to vanish at midnight.

The singing grew louder, and Ivy held her kids closer to her chest, vowing to protect them with every ounce of energy she had. When darkness descended on the tropics, it was thick, black, impenetrable in her blackness. In this rural town in those days, there was no electricity and no solar lights. Most people did not have money to buy kerosene for their Hurricane lamps. Most people simply put a piece of cloth into a jar of oil and lit it to provide just a tiny flicker of light. The darkness outside was only lit cold greenish miniature light of fireflies.

The commandos, as they called themselves, were eating and drinking at their commander's house. Rebel Madame made her way to the prison on foot. She wasn't thinking straight. Maybe the gin was using her as she became irrational, inserting the key into the prison armed with safety matches which she lit. Rebel Madame had the keys to the prison as she was the commander, and her men were out getting ready to come in an hour in a different way. The woman let out a loud shriek.

"Shhhsss," Rebel Madame put her fingers to her lips, signalling the woman to be quiet. Ivy recognized her as the one who outed her beloved Eddy as a soldier for him to be killed.

"Come with me quietly," Rebel Madame whispered. "And make it quick."

"I am not going anywhere with you, wicked woman," Ivy responded. "If you want to kill my children and me . . . do it right here and not in secret. You had my husband . . . ."

"Shsss," Rebel Madame tried to quiet her. "Please come with me. Any moment they will be here, and you will be gone. Come with me quickly and save yourself and your children."

"We aren't going anywhere," Ivy insisted.

"Listen in the distance, you will hear the singing," Rebel Madame said. "They are coming. Please come with me, for heaven's sake. If I wanted to kill you, I would have done so long ago. Come with me."

Something about the pleading in the voice of this notorious rebel fighter moved Ivy, and she grabbed the sleeping Willette and the wide-eyed Ebenezer.

"Mama, where are we going," Ebenezer asked.

"Ebenezer, please, for God's sake," Ivy whispered. "Follow me quietly, and don't ask any questions."

Rebel Madame grabbed Ivy's hands and led her through the dark streets of Vahun into the bushes.

"Halt!" A voice rang out at them. "Who's there?"

"Joe, come on, it's me, Rebel Madame."

"Rebel Madame, why aren't you at the C.O. house?"

Fighter Joe sounded a bit suspicious, but such was Rebel Madame's reputation and respect that when she said, "I will soon be on my way there for us to go and complete our mission," he did not come closer.

Furtively they made their way through the bushes using only a tiny torchlight.

The singing, dancing, bloodthirsty men burst through the prison gate and found an empty cell, and the pursuit began in earnest. The fugitive was an urban-born woman unaccustomed to the ways of the bush. Furthermore, she had young children to impede her progress toward the border. Once she crossed into Sierra Leone, she was safe.

Rebel Madame knew where all the checkpoints were. And just after midnight, she whispered to Ivy. "You see that tree there? It marks the boundary between Liberia and Sierra Leone. Go to safety with your children. One day Liberia will know peace, and this senseless war will be over. My family life was yanked from me, and I can't bear to see you lose your precious children and your own life. Go, tomorrow is another day when the sun will shine again."

"Please, Rebel Madame, come with us. My parents are in the United States, and they will help us. I will tell them how you saved our lives. Come with us."

There were sounds of approaching men walking and running like hoofbeats in the distance. The jungle was pitched black, and a thousand insects that lived to inflict pain while taking nutrients from one's body latched onto their skins. Miraculously, an angel closed Ebenezer and his young sister's mouths as they meandered their way with their mother through a barely visible footpath.

Rebel Madame laughed, and it was without mirth, and it was dry.

"I am a killer," she said. "And that's the life out there for me. Hurry up and go. I can hear the commandos coming."

Rebel Madame pushed Ivy across the border; then Ivy was into Sierra Leone.

Soon she heard screams and yelling and howling behind her.

"Rebel Madame, what the hell are you doing here," Young Killer asked.

Even as Young Killer asked the question, he knew the answer.

"So, you, of all people, help that devil and her children escaped," he asked incredulously.

Soon Rebel Madame was tied and dragged to rebel headquarters in Vahun. But she was a heroine of the Revolution. She had fought from Gborplay to Butuo and Karnplay and all the way here. Rebel Madame did not have a family; the people's popular uprising was all her family.

Rebel Madame was put into prison for a few days and released but told that if she ever made such an error again, she was going to pay for it with her life. Ivy and her kids strangely touched Rebel Madame. Dreams long suppressed and buried within her subconscious mind started to rear their ugly heads. Need I explain again?

Rebel Madame became Kou again. She went back to school and realized her dreams. She is a Nurse par excellence using her gifted hands to heal people somewhere in faraway Maryland County. Occasionally, she has nightmares about her days as Rebel Madame.

During a time of war, an innocent conversation with a friend can lead to dire unintended consequences. Cunning Johnson's voice can wiggle him out of most circumstances, but then again, will his sharp tongue deliver him from ruthless rebel anger?

My mouth will dump

It was very early Wednesday morning, the 28th day of March, and there were sounds of gunfire everywhere. A sustained burst of gunfire has never been experienced before. When the light of day appeared, men with Kalashnikov rifles and Berretta guns patrolled the streets. These men were armed with an odd assortment of weapons, including cutlasses and single-barrel guns, announcing that the Freedom Fighters have taken control. The areas they captured broke into rapturous joy. The people of the county welcome the rebels into their homes and towns. Were they not liberators driving the hated government and the much-despised government soldiers from the county? Did they not speak the same local languages? Were they not brothers, sisters, and cousins?

There were subtle differences, in any case. Most of the rebel fighters hailed from the more northern and eastern part of Nimba County and spoke with an accent different from the southerners from Tappeta. The rebel fighters from the early days of the war spoke with an accent more aligned to the Yacoubas from the Ivory Coast. The few rebel fighters from the south came with a chip on their shoulders. But soon, ordinary people began to realize that all that glitter was in no way gold. Rebel fighters carried a virulent hatred for anyone from a middle-class background and anyone who previously held any form of authority, no matter how minor in the government. Did everyone have to sit and await their arrival? Soon, the district's longest-serving paramount chief was held in a rebel prison. Was it not true that rebel commanders were demanding a hefty sum from his family in exchange for his freedom?

Was not Charles Snow, the former Magisterial court Judge, summarily executed by a rebel general because the general said many years ago, the judge delivered a judgment against his grandfather for a parcel of land? So now everyone had to be careful. Rebel commanders commandeer the best houses and the women they desired.

Johnson Tiatune was an avuncular personality and a civilian collaborator with the rebels. Johnson was dark complexioned with a strong, wiry beard, a pot belly, and a larger-than-life personality. He worked most of his life as a broadcaster with state radio, where his booming baritone voice as a language announcer was well known. He managed to take care of his two wives and one dozen children on his meager salary. Now he worked occasionally for a rebel radio station. The radio station was seized when white missionaries who built the radio station to propagate the gospel of Jesus Christ fled a few hours before rebels captured the isolated rural city. Now for a few hours in the evening, the station was on air broadcasting patriotic songs and flamboyant speeches from Charles Taylor, the CIC, as was known in rebel territory. Johnson Tiatune became the most popular announcer on rebel radio, using his well-modulated voice to urge support for what the rebels called people's popular uprising, aka Revolution. He didn't earn a salary, but the rebels paid him in rice and often shared loot from the battlefront as they advanced southwards to Buchanan.

While forces of the National Patriotic Front of Liberia advanced southward, Tappeta's temporary headquarters was not altogether safe. To supplement his earnings from unpaid work at the station, Johnson also worked the land as a farmer as he bided his time, waiting for a triumphal march into Monrovia. Once the rebels capture Monrovia and install themselves in power, he would be rewarded handsomely for his services to the Revolution. Just southwest of Tappeta, where Johnson had his rice farm, he and his two youngest sons stumbled across a contingent of Armed Forces of Liberia soldiers. No doubt these soldiers retreated from Tappeta and, planning what to do next, built a secret camp in the bush while strategizing on what to do next. From their position in the bush, crouched from where the soldiers could not see them, he counted about 10 soldiers. In shock, Johnson and his boys retreated without being seen.

Far away from the messengers of death, the teenagers, shaken and bewildered, turned to their dad.

"Papa, what are we going to do," they asked.

"I think we should immediately go to the town and report the matter to the freedom fighters. Didn't they say that when we see government soldiers, we should report the matter to them immediately?"

"True," Gontay's younger brother, Gontorwon, affirmed.

Johnson lapsed for a moment into deep thought while the boys waited in anticipation.

"Boys, listen," he said. "We must be careful. What if we tell the freedom fighters that we saw a group of soldiers, and they follow us here, and by the time we get here, the soldiers have fled? Never mind, I talk on their radio, and everyone knows me; I could be tortured as well as the both of you."

"Wow, I didn't think of that," said one of the sons. "Then we will be in deep shit. The freedom fighters will brand us government collaborators."

"So, sons, you see why we must seal our lips and keep our mouths shut when we leave from here. Do you understand me, boys," Johnson added, placing his pointing fingers, sealing his lips.

"But dad, what if the soldiers' counterattack and kill people," Gontay asked.

"Gontay, you sound like a child. If the AFL could not defend their barracks when the freedom fighters attacked, would a small band of 10 soldiers dare counterattack? In a day or two, those guys will be finding their way back into government territory. We just stumbled upon them by mistake. Tomorrow they will be gone. When we leave here, don't say a word to a soul. Not to your mother or friends. Am I clear?"

"Yes, Papa."

This was still rural Africa in the early 1990s when a man ruled his home with an iron fist. If only Johnson Tiatune had kept his own counsel, it would have been well.

Sadly, Johnson Tiatune did not keep his own counsel. The monstrosity of what he and his sons saw could not stay with him. However, his penchant for sharing information overcame his better judgment, and he narrated the story to Guva, his best friend, who was known as a discreet family man.

Two days later, Johnson Tiatune was sitting with his large family sharing a meal and having a laugh with his kids in the suburb of Gibson Town. It was a fantastic breezy evening and a good one because earlier, his daughters had a successful day fishing in the creeks and had brought some fish. It surprised Johnson that his daughters, born in the city, were adapting to rural life in these difficult times. Leamon and Zaye even bought good-quality cane juice for their dad.

It was one of those evenings a man wished to live his entire life for—fun and quality family time in a gregarious household. Jonson was taking a sip from his favorite gin bottle when he lifted his head; to his utmost surprise, shock, and bewilderment, spied his friend, Guva, walking towards his house, followed by five young NPFL soldiers. Their hands appeared perilously close to the trigger. In authentic rebel styles, they wore red bandanas on their foreheads along with an odd assortment of female hair wigs. The gun magazines were tied together with black adhesive tapes.

Instantly, Johnson Tiatune knew what had happened. He was about to be tied, beaten, and paraded before the town. Worst, all the humiliation was going to happen right before his family and children; never mind, he was a prominent broadcaster for the rebels who insisted on being called freedom fighters. That was going to be the case if he took the NPFL fighters to the site where he and his sons stumbled upon the soldiers, and if the soldiers in the bush had fled, which he knew was the case, all hell would break loose for him.

His mind was spinning in a circle, and soon not only his mind but his physical being was in a circle of five freedom fighters and his good friend, Guva.

"We are not here to waste time," a dark and lankly teenager appeared to be the group's leader. "Speak up. What did you say your friend told you about Doe Soya and where are they, eh?"

All the men who had come refused to be seated. Johnson's wife and daughters hurried inside the house with the younger kids, shrieking and wailing in fright.

"My. . . my friend here," Guva stammered.

Johnson could not believe his eyes and ears that his friend could betray him so badly.

"My friend, Johnson, tells me the day before yesterday, he saw about ten Doe Soya (A derogatory term for AFL soldiers) not far from here on his farm," Guva finished. "That's what he tells me. But anyway, da na me who see the soldiers dem. Da Johnson, so he can explain what he saw. I'm only doing this so we all can be safe."

"Ok, Mr. Johnson! Come with us right away to the brigade headquarters."

"Hold on, wait. Let the Papay explain first. After that, then we can take him to the C.O. for him to carry us where he saw de soya dem," one of the men said.

"True, my pekin, you talk sense," said the leader. "Let Pa Tiatune explain what he saw. Papay, I am Commander Bumie. Talk quickly because we are ready for you to take us where you saw the soldiers. And pray to God the soyas are still there because if we don't see them, you will feel severe pain for lying to us."

Johnson broke into an almost hysterical burst of laughter that stunned everyone present and bewildered them all at once. What was this man laughing for? This was a matter of life and death. Well, pretty soon, his laughter will turn to gravel in his mouth.

An impatient rebel fighter took his gun to hit the laughing Johnson with his gun butt. But surprisingly, commander Bumie stayed his hand as they all waited for Johnson to calm down. And even when he did, everyone could see how hard he was trying not to laugh again.

"You know, Commander Bumie, I cannot believe how stupid my friend here, Guva, standing before you and your friends can be," Johnson said. "I know you commandos are very busy and serious people that came to free us. I can't believe my friend dared to waste your precious time that could be used for doing something more useful."

Johnson broke into a burst of laughter again.

"I cannot believe in my wildest imagination that Guva could waste your time on the mere account of a dream," Johnson said. "I was explaining to my friend here a dream. In my dream, some of the AFL soldiers who ran away from Tappeta were camping on the Buchanan highway. The dream looked real, and sweat was pouring down my body when I woke up later. The good thing is, while those fools were eating and drinking, a group of freedom fighters came across them, and there was a brief firefight in which all the soldiers were killed. I can call my wife here now, and she can explain this exact dream to you. Pillar!" Johnson shouted his wife's name.

This was a high-risk strategy. Although Johnson knew his head wife could not contradict him, he prayed that she heard his narration from inside and repeated just what he narrated.

"I didn't tell him anything about soldiers being on my farm," Johnson continued. "If I, Johnson Tiatune, saw any soldier or even smell them near me, I would be the one running to make a report to your freedom fighters."

Johnson began laughing almost uncontrollably again as the rebel freedom fighters, so quick to resort to senseless barbarity, stood in stupefied silence, unsure of what to do.

"I can't believe Guva could just waste the time of our beloved freedom fighters," Johnson said. "Incredible!"

The silence of the fighters dissipated, replaced by the emotions that came naturally to them. Anger and an affinity for violence. Blows and gun butts came crashing down on Guva.

"Do you think we are here to play," the commander shouted. "Do we look like toys to you? Your friend tells you his dream, then you come to us with a lie?"

He landed a blow on Guva's face as he attempted to explain.

"If you open your dirty mouth, I will shoot you," a rebel fighter screamed. "Haven't you wasted our time enough today. . . bringing us here because of a dream."

"Tie the man up," the commander ordered. "Let's take him to the C.O. for the chief to determine what will happen to him."

"Sorry, Pa Tiatune," one soldier said. "We are so sorry."

Guva was thrown into the back of a pick-up, and they drove away, through the dusty streets of Tappeta, to meet the C.O.

The writer is unsure of what happened to Guva at the time of writing this story, but Johnson was glad his quick thinking and natural flair for acting saved

him from humiliation and possible death. Johnson
lived long to see the end of the war and now works at
the Ministry of Information, where he still narrates
this story with a twink of glee in his ears all these years
later because all ends well.

A young man, a young woman, and a young daughter. Love and family are the last things we all hold dear. Miatay and Yiley are poor and very much in love. Then Yiley emigrates to Australia for resettlement. Even from afar, they longed to be reunited. And when they do, it is a glorious moment. But can love always remain steadfast in a developed country?

He won't come back to me

Miatay had never been crammed within a specific place for hours, high above the vast, almost unending sea.

"Sir, what would you like to have," the flight attendant asked. "Coffee, tea, biscuits, snacks, or alcohol?"

Miatay smiled weakly at the tall white woman standing before him. Her hair was neatly combed back and tied with a red band that matched her lipstick and red dress. A colorful red sash adorned her dress. Miatay, a black African man who had grown up in the heavily forested country of Liberia, had never been served by a white woman until today, let alone be called *Sir* by one. He was indeed headed to a new life. He simply stared at her.

"Sir, what would you like," she asked again, smiling.

Mesmerized, Miatay responded in a barely audible voice with his thick Liberian accent, "Thank you."

"I beg your pardon."

"Thank you . . . I am fine," Miatay said, nodding his head just in case the flight attendant did not understand his accent.

She moved along the aisle, offering the same goodies to another passenger, who gladly accepted.

Miatay could not wait to get off the plane. He had heard that Australia was far away. Now he was on a plane, the third aircraft on his journey; he could not believe how far away Australia was. A mixture of fear and excitement kept him away throughout the long trip from Guinea Conakry on an Air France flight to Charles De Gaulle airport in Paris. The transit in Paris was 15 hours.

He could not get over the clean, crystal-white toilet. One could sit on the floor and eat. Mirrors lined the face basin, and when one went to use the washer, the automatic sprinklers sprayed water onto one's hand. Miatay was startled when the water came unto his hands. He regained his composure and smiled. He was in a developed country, and his excitement bubbled like a kid in a candy store.

From Paris, Miatay and his young daughter, who got the lion's share of the hostesses' attention, flew to Hong Kong first, and now they were finally on a Qantas flight bound for Australia.

He tried falling asleep but found it impossible to close his eyes. He was afraid of heights and the aircraft, yet excited beyond belief. Holding Yiley in his arms again would mean the world to him. Flashbacks of their times together splashed across his eyes and blew sleep away. All he could hear was the loud hump sound of the airbus tearing its way through the endless cloud. Then after what seemed like an eternity, he heard the words he now, in the past 48 hours or so, have grown accustomed to.

"This is the captain speaking. Fasten your seatbelts. The weather in Melbourne is . . . Cabin crew prepare for landing."

The voice echoed over the plane's PA system. The flight attendants were making their final inspection for landing, telling a passenger to straighten their seat, another to open a window blind, and another to fasten his seat belt.

Then Australia appeared beneath the plane, and Miatay felt the thud noise of the airplane hitting the tarmac. Soon they landed, and when the plane door opened, a blast of chilly air hit him with such force and intensity he had never imagined. His teeth began to chatter immediately. *How could a place be so cold?*

Where in the world was Australia? Was it a country? A continent. Yiley knew there were animals with long hind legs and short stumps for hands that hopped around in a faraway country. Every Liberian wanted to emigrate to America, the land of Burger Kings,

Coca-Cola, and big houses and cars. But what was this place called Australia? Some people said it was a place so desperately short of black people to work on their farms that they were getting farm laborers under the guise of refugees' resettlement. Others said Australia was so far away that the sun did not set when one lived there because it was the world's end.

Rumors swelled around Camp Laine, a sprawling refugee camp deep in the jungles of the Forest Region of Guinea, far away from the capital and other major urban settlements. White and green tarpaulin structures built in neat, orderly roles edged into the distance as far as the eyes could see.

In this artificial town carved out of the jungle to host people fleeing wars from Liberia, Ivory Coast, and Sierra Leone, Yiley lived with her common-law husband, Miatay, sharing a single bedroom with their three-year-old daughter, Vonyee. Life was a hard affair in this camp, with very few employment opportunities and isolation from the world. There was no internet, mobile phone coverage or electricity. But there was good tap water, a makeshift MSF hospital that offered reasonably good health services, a school and other non-governmental organisation that provided everything from sanitation to food. An assortment of do-gooders from western countries helped make the drudgery and despondency in the camp a little better and even cosy for some. Sometimes locals resented all the attention paid to the refugees.

Unlike their relatively well-off neighbours who often received money and support from relatives in

America, Miatay and Yiley had no one overseas. They fled Ganta during intense battles for the city in 2003 between LURD rebels and government forces, running only with the clothes on their back, making their way to Guinea and Camp Laine.

Miatay did not have a job in the camp, neither did Yiley. Miatay earned money by doing odd carpentry jobs for friends and neighbours. Yiley did not fare better. She often did 'sell pay' business selling fish in the small camp market since most people in the camp often went to Laine Town, not far from the camp where local Guineans live to do their shopping. Yiley did not have money to buy the fish she sold retail; she took the fish from fish mongers in Laine Town, sold the fish and returned the fishmonger's money while pocketing the little profit earned for herself and her family. What the young couple and their daughter lacked in material things, they more than made up for in love. Yiley was an exceedingly attractive woman in her mid-twenties with dark skin that glistered under the tropical sun. When she smiled, her milky white burst out, shining like a goddess. Miatay, in his late twenties, with good looks, a round face, developed muscular physique, and curly jet-black hair could easily make women swoon with his roguish good looks. In what some may consider strange, the couple had only eyes for each other, and there was no sense of unfaithfulness. They did not marry in the western tradition so favoured by young Liberian women and, to a lesser extent, men with the long glowing white wedding dress, rings, bridesmaids, groomsmen and smartly dressed kids serving as ring bearers. They were too poor to afford that.

Miatay Uncle met Yiley's uncle, paid the bride price, and gave Yiley away. There was a war going on in Liberia, and only Yiley's mother managed to come to Guinea. Yiley's dad was fighting LURD in Ganta, and as a frontline commander, he did not have the chance to leave his men to attend his daughter's wedding. Both Miatay's parents were deceased. And then one-day, Yiley's name appeared on the UNHCR women at risk program because a couple of months ago, Yiley registered for some program targeting vulnerable women at risk in the camp. The aid worker told Yiley not to mention Miatay because that might jeopardise her travel opportunities. True to the aid worker's words within of participating in the women at risk survey, Yiley was on her way to Australia like a whirlwind and resettled in Brisbane, the glittering city with a sub-tropical climate that served as the capital city for the state of Queensland.

When one loves the fast and frenetic pace of life with teeming crowds, you go to Sydney. When a person love class and culture, the place to be was Melbourne with its cosmopolitan liberal outlook and cold climate. The pace of life in Brisbane, Australia's third largest city, was more relaxed yet offered the variety of big city life and a friendly country town feeling. It was this city Yiley settled in, assisted by church-run resettlement agencies who found accommodation for her in the inner-city suburb of Coorparoo. Coorparoo was less than 15 minutes' drive to the city centre and had many different bus routes making public transport readily available. Her townhouse was one of those late 70s, and early 80s blocked-style apartments of made of sun-dried bricks and steep stairs. Although in later years, Yiley would recognise the condo as being stuffy and boxlike, in those early years, the neat, clean apartment filled with modern appliances like a refrigerator, microwave, cookers, washing machine, television and comfortable second-hand chairs looked like paradise. Clean, air-conditioned buses and trains that run on time. Glittering shopping malls like Queen Street mall dazzled her and made her thank the Lord for letting her, a girl who grew up in the country to become a resident in Australia.

Notwithstanding the cold weather and the difficult to understand English, and her having to repeat her words twice or even three times before Australians understood what she said, there was euphoria in being in Australia. The fridge was always full of food, and she got free money from Centrelink, which she sent most to friends and family in Africa. Being around so many white people seemed so strange to her. Sometimes riding the train to Southbank in the city, it was eerie being the only black person on board. But human beings get used to things. Apart from the occasional stare or out-of-place condescending words, Yiley found Australians generally friendly and hospitable. In a few short months, she would say an occasional word that sounded like them, and when she got her Certificate111 in Aged Care to go and take care of old people in a retirement home, it was a significant milestone, just like when she got her driver's license a week later.

The work was hard, and shift work sometimes made her feel tired. But the pay was good, and for the first time in her life, Yiley felt good making money and buying things she could only dream of a year ago. She bought herself a small Mazda car and drove herself to work. Stones Corner, with her specialty shops and banks, was 10 minutes' walk from her house. A friend of hers, Lydia, informed her that there were shops in Moorooka that sold African food, jewellery, and clothes. Furthermore, most of the shop owners were African, and she could see people who looked like her. She soon learned of a Liberian organisation that catered to the Liberian community in Queensland, of which she became a part.

Despite the progress, Yiley was making, she felt a terrible loneliness which had never experienced before. She missed Miatay terribly. His laughter, his charm, his lovemaking, and everything about him. Her young daughter, whom she could not bring because she was with her grandma, she missed all the time. While she could occasionally catch up with friends in person or on the phone, she thought most of the friendships in Brisbane were shallow. She spent a good sum of money on phone cards to talk to her husband and her young daughter. While her friends talked excitedly about new boyfriends, she only spoke about Miatay, which sometimes annoyed her free-spirited friends. "Husband in Africa indeed," her friends sneered. "Don't enjoy yourself with the hot guys here black and white instead of waiting for a guy in Africa who might leave you when he comes here. Do you know what your wonderful Miatay is doing in Africa? Maybe spending the money, you sent to him on new girlfriends."

Such talk was hurtful to Yiley, so she tried her best to avoid Yamah, Kolu, and Kemah. They did not know who Miatay was, so they did not know what they were talking about. In no time, Yiley developed a reputation of being a committed married woman. It was hard, but she was determined to behave differently from what she saw around her.

July 26, Liberia's Independence Day celebrations took her to Sydney for the first time. The Sydney opera house made her to give a yell, but there was something else. On the steps of the iconic structure, she saw a figure she knew very well and did not know was in Australia. And she ran to him unabashed in her excitement.

There was Daniel, Miatay's best friend from the camp! Gone were the tawdry and lanky skeletal structure but a full-figure man looking dapper. At last, there was someone whom she could incessantly about Miatay with a hint of malice. There was so much to talk about. She ran into his arms.

"Oh, Daniel my God."

"Yiley, is that you? When did you come to Australia? Which state are you in?"

He bombarded her as he embraced Yiley tightly.

"Where is Miatay? Is he here with you?"

"No not yet."

"And where is my friend Sandra?"

"Not here yet."

What happiness it brought to Yiley to speak to someone she could speak so freely about her love and the things dearest to her heart without hearing snide comments. From the Opera House, Yiley and Daniel, along with the others in the group, took a double-decked train to central. This was a massive train station with 26 platforms and an endless stream of people appearing in all sizes, colours, and creeds hurried along in a constant cacophony of motion up and down escalators and stairs. Massive trains travelling in all directions, including to the country, decked the station. The group took the train to the western suburbs where most immigrants to Sydney live. To sightsee better, the group hopped onto the upper floor and swing the twin seated leather seats to the directions out west. The train was crowded, and the voice announcing departure blared on the PA system.

That night Yiley and Daniel talked late into the night. Yiley spoke freely about how she missed Miatay so much that her heart ached for him. How her friends mocked her for daring her to be faithful to Miatay instead of getting boyfriends or travelling from state to state enjoying the late parties of Adelaide, Melbourne, Sydney, and other places. And a sympathetic ear Daniel was because of Miatay's best friend.

It was moving. Daniel spoke of his love and deep affection for his wife Sandra and how she looked forward with eager anticipation for their resettlement in Australia, a process which he had started already with the Department of Home Affairs. By the time the money came, there was a deep bond of solidarity between the two.

When the July 26 celebrations ended, and Yiley returned to Brisbane, she had a spring in her steps. She narrated the encounter with Daniel to Yiley, and down the long-distance phone line, Miatay shouted, his voice reeking with excitement. Yiley's life returned to her work routine and the process of bringing Miatay and their young daughter to Australia. Occasionally she spoke to Daniel on the phone, but nothing beyond that.

August 24th celebrations, there was a ball celebrating Liberia's Flag Day at the Serbian Hall in Willawong in the southwestern suburbs of Brisbane. Previously an industrial suburb, Brisbane's recent population growth had led to housing complexes in Pallara, Heathwood, Inala, and other adjacent suburbs. Dressed in a flowing red gown Yiley was literally dragged to the program honouring the flag with the hall decked in red, white, and blue, the national colours. Soft music played in the background as young models. Cat walked to the applause of the audience.

Sipping wine, Yiley lifted her head she saw him in a dark suit with white shirt. He looked dapper and dashing like an image of a Greek god.

"Daniel!"

He smiled and said, "I did not know you will be here."

"I had to come since you stopped picking up my call."

And then the dreaded words came out.

"Yiley, I want you as a lover. I can't beat around the bush anymore."

The garbage coming out of Daniel's mouth were sacrilegious. Yiley was not angry but astounded.

"How could you say that...but he is your best friend and Sandra is my best friend."

Yiley heard herself saying as if she was half conscious.

"I am not telling you to leave my best friend. I am not saying I will leave Sandra. Matter of fact I love Sandra. But even you cannot deny the incredible attraction between us two. So who else to take good care of my best friend's wife except me?"

Yiley was quiet.

"I am not saying leave my friend, I am just asking for us to help each other, friends with benefit, and when our respective spouses come, we can stop being lovers and go back to them."

Could this handsome man stop spewing such garbage? Yiley wanted to throw up. Her mind screamed no, but her body was not sure. She was so lonely and truly liked him, but she could not betray Miatay. In a daze, Yiley manoeuvred her car out of the outdoor parking through Archerfield Road into the city.

Days later, Yiley encountered Daniel in a shop in Moorooka, and he offered to help put her new bed up, which the company had delayed doing that. Why did she tell Daniel?

When she did, and Daniel offered his help, Yiley could not refused.

From that day, they became lovers to Yiley's astonishment, horror, and pleasure.

Miatay could see his body moving. His mind did not cooperate much with him. The combination of lack of sleep, food, and excitement took its toll.

An IOM representative helped him clear customs and passport control quickly. But Miatay had no passport, only his IOM bag and a document issued by the Australian government to travel to Australia. Yiley's hair plaited with attachment was tied with a blue ribbon at the back, gently flowing to her back. She had put on a bit of weight but was in no way fat. Her whole body, black and beautiful, glistened more in the bright fluorescent light at the airport's waiting area. The red lipstick cleverly pencil made her look radiant. The vestiges of poverty had left this attractive young woman, and she blossomed in this strange land. There she was waiting for him Miatay forgot about his young daughter holding his arm and knocking his thigh for attention as he stood mesmerised by his wife's beauty.

In contrast, he looked skinny and famished by comparison. There she was running towards him, and he lengthened his strides, eventually breaking into a run. The two lovers embraced with all the longing heart, and satisfaction that could exist between two people scooping their daughter up simultaneously. Yiley drove leisurely from the airport through the leafy suburbs along the riverfront down Fortitude

Valley into the southern part of Brisbane. Yiley and another friend accompanied her to the airport. In the big, spacious house filled with glittering furniture, Miatay kept staring, almost lost for words. He was mesmerised by his wife's beauty, and his love for her swelled. Baked chicken, fried greens and potatoes, salad, beer, wine, and everything.

When night came, Miatay and Yiley lay in bed for the first time in five years and were still talking. And when his arms went around her body, she gently pushed him away, saying there would be more than enough time for that. Then the next night and the next. Night merged into days and days into the night. Yiley took him shopping at Carindale Shopping centre, and was extremely pleasant to him, but the intimacy he yearned for was always tomorrow.

In public, Yiley introduced him as her baby daddy and never her husband. When they attended church, his wife kept busy talking to other people, only joining him when there was time only to start the car and drive away.

Miatay danced when Daniel invited him to his place at Redbank Plains further west of Coorparoo. The two friends hugged, and over cold bottles of beer, they reminisced about their younger days in Africa playing Football and hustling for food to eat in the evening hours. Daniel even offered to help him find a job with one disability agency he worked with. Daniel drove Miatay home late in the night and gave him $200 for pocket money. Daniel drove Miatay straight to his house.

That was not strange. Yiley told him Daniel visited her once or twice.

Yiley was in turmoil.

Matters of the heart do not go the way of the mind. Last night she allowed Miatay to enjoy his marital right in bed. And she realised that she must face reality stark naked and brutal in its manifestation. She could not hide from herself anymore. The realisation was cruel and unthinkable.

She was in love with Daniel!

How could she say this to Miatay without breaking his heart or losing her sanity? She fought against herself and her irrational irreverent feelings in the days that followed. She blocked Daniel's number from her phone a week after Miatay's arrival because he had been calling incessantly for them to have a secret rendezvous pulling at the strains of her heart. Tried as she did, her body felt no affection for Miatay anymore. Finally, after struggling with herself for a month, and the feelings would not go away, Yiley decided to grab the bull by the horn one night while their young daughter slept in her room. Miatay, her young husband, snored beside her. Each time she made up her mind to tell him what was torturing her mind, she felt back into bed sleepless, staring at the ceiling.

Finally, she tapped him, and he groaned, turning over. Yiley tapped Miatay's shoulders with a bit of force until he woke up leaning on a paper.

"What is it baby? I am so tired from working in the chicken factory. I am not used to such hard work."

"I know baby and feel for you. But there is something I need to tell you."

"Can't it wait till tomorrow? Baby, I really need to sleep since I return to work in the morning."

"No, it can't wait." The insistent tone in Yiley's voice made sleep to suddenly vanish from his eyes.

"Ok baby go on I am listening. I just don't understand why the urgency though."

"There is something I need to tell you. But I don't know how to start or how to say it."

"Then do not say it."

"But I must!"

"Alright go on."

"You know Miatay you have been a good husband to me, and I love you. I can record in a vivid way all the hard time we went through in the camp. I can remember when my footwear cut and you fashioned a pair of footwear out of your shirt. And what lousy slipper it was."

"But it did help you."

They both burst out laughing.

Then Yiley became serious again.

"Ever since you arrived in this country, I have been miserable."

"Why baby, we have been happy."

"I only pretended to be."

Then she burst out screaming.

"Miatay, I don't love you anymore. I have tried so hard to love you and be a dutiful wife to you. I am tired pretending. I love someone else and don't love you anymore and can't be your wife. I sent money already for my parents to return your bride price to your family. Since Australia recognise us as defacto, we do not need to go through a civil divorce here. I don't love and can't be your wife anymore."

"You said you love someone else. And who is that person?"

Then it dawned on Miatay.

"It is Daniel, right?"

Yiley did not answer. She burst out sobbing, and then everything went blue and green in Miatay's eyes. When he woke up there were tubes all over Miatay at the Queen Elizabeth Jubilee Hospital. Miatay wanted to die. Deep depression like never before in his life descended on him. Images and videos on their happy life together played continuously in his mind. This new world that was supposed to bring him happiness has been unnecessarily cruel to him, and he wanted no part of it. Miatay was ashamed of going back to Africa and to imagine his best friend taking away his wife while he was powerless, in a strange land without many friends and support network; life meant nothing to him except perhaps his daughter. Maybe it was good for his daughter if his useless life was snatched away. Deep darkness descended upon Miatay. Feeling betrayed, hopeless, and worthless, he could not see beyond the dense fog. Miatay yearned for the good old days, but they were gone and never to come again. He willed himself to think of the past, hoping that somehow, through his willpower, the past could transform into the present. Friends who pitied him could occasionally hear 'I want go back to Africa" in his incoherent rant with Yiley's name being repeated on his lips.

When he was discharged from the hospital, Miatay did not care whether he lived. The President of the Liberian Association and a group of women stayed with him cooking for him, talking to him and just being available for him. Food had no taste in his mouth and all he wanted was to drink, to drink so that he could numb his mind and not remember. Even people who took pity on him became restless and fed up, but strangers from the Liberian community stayed with him. The kindness of strangers gradually made him to grow stronger. One of them an ethnic Muslim from the north of Liberia, introduced him to his boss at the Ingham Chicken Factory where he worked at Murarrie near the port of Brisbane where he worked and got Miatay on the same shift he worked so he could drive Miatay to and from work. When Miatay got his first pay packet, he could not believe the amount. Nearly $2,000. He eventually got his driver's license which was a rite of passage for anyone resettled in Australia and bought himself a Toyota.

Yiley heart missed a beat when Miatay finally left her house so she could be with the man who stole his heart. She and Daniel visited the glitz and glamour of a penthouse hotel on the Gold Coast and even visited Noosa. Life was good and blissful, and it seemed life could not get better than this.

Six months later, Yiley was troubled. Daniel informed her that his wife Sandra and their three kids' visa had been approved, and they were enroute to Australia. Daniel sounded excited as he breathlessly narrated.

"I can't believe after 5 long years Sandra and the kids will be finally here. Oh my God the kids will finally go to school, eat regularly, and enjoy. Sandra is just one patient woman and God is rewarding her patience."

"Ok, good for you."

Yiley's voice sounded more like a whisper than a comment as she tried to control the anger bursting inside.

Veronica had average good looks and was in no way stunningly beautiful as Yiley. But she possessed exceptional intelligence and was loving a kind. From being an aged care worker, she studied and worked her way to becoming an Enrolled Nurse at Aveo Aged Care facility in Oxley in the western suburbs of Brisbane in Oxley along Blunder Road. And she showed that kindness to Miatay. It wasn't love at first sight. It was a slow-burning candle, and some irresistible force drew the two young people together. They slowly over time became a couple known for their dedication and hard work. They soon began investing in real estate buying their first house in Ipswich and a second investment property in Crestmead in Logan.

"So your family is coming, and you are happy, right?"

"Of course, what do you reckon? Isn't Sandra, your friend and you should be happy for her?"

"Happiness, my foot. What becomes of me? You know because of you I left Miatay. What becomes of me?"

"Did I asked you to leave Miatay? We both knew were only helping each other until our respectively partners come."

"And what in God's name were you calling and texting me when Miatay came? Do you think I am some old piece of cloth you can use and throw away when your family comes?"

"Oh, I am not throwing you away. We can still be lovers, but you must know Sandra and the kids come first."

"So, I will be your side chick waiting at your beck and call the day Sandra is not around?"

"We both knew what we were getting into."

That was too much for Yiley. Daniel's arrogance was beyond her, and she grabbed a bottle and whacked him on the head, and an ambulance was called to take Daniel to the hospital and the police took Yiley away to the Acacia Ridge police station.

Last I heard, Sandra and her three children are living in Brisbane with their husband and dad. Daniel's forehead has a slight, albeit it prominent scar on his forehead. Daniel refused to press charges against Yiley. They no longer speak.

Miatay and Veronica have a kid, and they are talking of marriage. Everyone who knows them speaks highly of them as a solid, hard-working couple. Miatay and Yiley's daughter is now a teenager, and she speaks so much, similar to the Australian kid next door that everyone thinks she was born in Australia.

Yiley is back in love with Miatay and calls him incessantly, saying she has a revelation that God wants them to be back together so he can do a brand-new thing in their lives.

This story is enigmatic. A man betrayed his boss by arresting him and turning him over for prosecution or death. This story is based on an incident in Liberia's history in 1985. General Thomas Quiwonkpa and his Patriotic Forces invaded Liberia to launch a coup. The story is, however, a work of fiction, although two of the main protagonists in the story are historical figures in Liberia. Adolphus Kaykar, the bodyguard to powerful Liberia's Immigration Service chief Cornelius Tate, arrested his boss and handed him over to the coup makers. When the coup fails, Chief Cornelius vows his revenge on Adolphus. At this crucial time Adolphus's father intervenes to save his life.

My son will live for me

The old man looked ordinary, wearing a pair of blue rubber slippers and a black Fezzan cap covering his bald head. He wore simple black flowing ropes and carried a small brown wooden walking stick. His command of the English language was poor because he mastered speaking a distinct dialect spoken in the thick tropical forest that marked the boundaries of Nimba, Grand Gedeh, Grand Bassa, and Ri/cess counties. The language he spoke was similar to Krahn linguistically but borrowed many words from the Bassa ethnic group. Even in underdeveloped Liberia, this part of Liberia where the old man hailed from was on another level of underdevelopment without a single paved road, electricity, hospital, or high school. His people lived in isolated towns and homesteads scattered in the deep lush tropical vegetation of central Liberia. His people were also master herbalists, and traditional African fetish religion still held strong sway over them in addition to Christianity. Physically they were short race; height in the forest was a disadvantage rather than an advantage as venomous snakes, insects, and plants covered the upper echelons of the forest. Whereas tall height made a person susceptible to insect and snake bites and thorns, a short physical structure enabled them to be nimble on their feet.

Elite guards of the Special Anti-Terrorist Unit SATU soldiers guarding the Executive Mansion held their breath in bewilderment, bafflement, and hilarious contempt when a traditional man wearing beads around his neck and a small black plastic bag under his arms materialized out of nowhere. He looked ornery; there was nothing impressive or dignified about him. His lean figure and weather-beaten face showed his peasant ancestry and long hours spent working under the sun. From nowhere, he emerged and stood at the entrance of the imposing Presidential palace, saying he came to see the President. The bafflement and contempt of the young soldiers turned to intrigue.

"Papay, who are you?"

"My name is old man Varmie, and I came to see the President, Samuel Doe?"

"Are you related to the President?"

"No."

"Does he have an appointment with you?"

"No."

"Is the President expecting you?"

"No."

"Why do you want to see the President?"

"I won't tell anyone why I want to see the President until I meet him face to face."

"Face to face about what?"

"My son."

"Your son? Who's your son?"

"I won't say another word unless I see the President," the old man said defiantly.

The soldiers were exasperated, amused, and then intrigued at the simple-looking countryman from the interior who refused to leave their checkpoint, saying he would only go after he'd met with the President. When the soldiers became exasperated and threatened to beat him up if he did not leave their checkpoint, he simply relocated across the road to the Capitol Building side, where he could see right into the Mansion's fence while ensuring he remained within the vision of the cracked soldiers.

By midday, Captain Thomas Doe, a cousin of the President, tired of watching the old man, walked to the top floor of the Mansion where the President was.

"Cousin, you won't believe what is happening downstairs," he said to the President.

Sitting beside the President was the powerful deputy commissioner of Immigration, Cornelius Taye, and a host of others hailing from the President's home county. The powerful Minister of Justice and a coterie of relations from cousins to nephews and nieces, who made up the core of his inner cabinet ministers, sat around the President. President Doe listened to these men's advice more than his cabinet ministers.

The President sat upright, folding his arm and placing the bottom half of his elbow on the table. He was young with a ruggedly handsome and rotund face.

"There is this old man downstairs who says his name is Varmie; he said he came to Monrovia purposely to see you. I asked him if he was related to you or had an appointment with you. He says no. He wants to talk to you and no one else about his son. He refuses to leave and has been sitting there all day."

The faces of the President and his advisers vacillated, showing utter bewilderment and amusement.

"Mr. President, I can make him disappear without a trace," Daniel said. "What kind of crappy old man just came out of nowhere demanding to see you? He could be a witch doctor armed with some powerful voodoo to bewitch you and your advisers. I could shoot him on the spot."

"Shut the f—k up. Daniel, it's you, always trigger-happy and only too eager to spill blood. Captain Thomas, go and escort the man to me. Frisk him and make sure he does not have any charms on him."

"What?"

The look of aghast expression on the faces of everyone expressed their thoughts more eloquently than words.

The short, dark-skinned man with a short stubble of grey hair spoke straight without candor or sophistication, still refusing to part with his plastic bag containing a shirt and a black pair of trousers when he was brought upstairs to see the President. The opulent surroundings of the office of the President seemed to make him feel a bit ill at ease. He glanced at the many unfamiliar beautiful things and then focused his gaze intensely on the face of the President.

"Mr. President, as you can see, I am a simple countryman who did not go to school. I don't like this place where human beings fall over one another like driver ants. I do not intend to stay a day longer than necessary in this city. As soon as you grant my request, I will leave this city and will never return to it until the day I die. My request is simple. Free my son, Adolphus Kaykar, whom I heard is detained by you."

The President looked stunned.

"Who is Adolphus Kaykar," President Doe asked. "I've never heard of such a man."

"Mr. President, remember my chief bodyguard whom I told you handcuffed and arrested me the morning of November 12," Commissioner Tate said, then paused for effect. "On the day of the aborted invasion . . . the morning of November 12," he resumed. "This traitor arrested me and handed me over to the rebels at the BTC Barracks to be killed."

The President furrowed his brows and squinted his eyes. He grunted as if he had remembered something, shaking his head.

"Oldman Varmie, I thought I could help you, but even if I wanted to, your son's case is beyond redemption," President Doe said. "How could your son so ungraciously bite the hands that fed him in an ultimate act of betrayal?"

"Mr. President, this man, Adolphus, lived with me in my house for years," Commissioner Tate said. "He selected and ironed the clothes I wore. He tasted my food before I ate. My children called him *uncle*. If I came from work and saw him alone with my wife in my bedroom, I won't even think about anything amiss. My thoughts would be he went to ask my wife about me. Such was the level of trust I had in Adolphus. I could not believe that this man would be the one arresting me, humiliating, and taking me to the hands of my enemies at the BTC Barracks where Quiwonkpa and his accursed rebels were."

"Umm," Doe mumbled.

"Adolphus ordered me to undress, leaving me only in my underclothes," Commissioner Tate continued. "I swear I thought my life had ended. And there was Adolphus after he handed me over, sitting in my chair, taking over my office, and driving my car like he was me. I thought I had his loyalty. Instead, I got his envy and disloyalty. In this matter, life for life and death for death. I am sorry, Mr. Varmie."

"You heard the man," President Doe said to the old man. "I support what Commissioner Tate has said . . . hundred percent. I will ensure your son gets his just reward. Sit a minute, and we will show you evidence of your son's guilt."

A VCR tape was inserted into a 21-inch sharp television in the room. The grainy footage showed Adolphus Kaykar ordering his men to grab his boss and then he, himself, clanging the handcuff on Commissioner Tate's hand behind his back.

Mr. Varmie sat impassively at first, listening to Commissioner Tate and then the President. He watched the incriminating video recording of his son engaging in a despicable act of betrayal and said nothing.

After a pause, the old man spoke in his direct, matter-of-fact way.

"Look, Mr. President, I did not come here to plead my son's innocence. I came to ask you for mercy. My son is young and foolish. Foolishness is bound in the heart of a child. If my son was wise, why would he choose to align himself with a bunch of ragtag rebel invaders whom he wasn't even sure for one second their plans would succeed? I know you are a wise man. Somehow you may have heard Quiwonkpa and his men were coming, and you were prepared for that. My foolish son knew nothing of those things. So, he jumped in without thinking. Now he knows which side of his bread has butter. The good thing is when you free him, he will swear an oath of allegiance to you and Commissioner Tate with his blood and mine. And until his dying breath, he will serve you faithfully. The Gbis and the Krahns are kinsfolks. My son did not understand this. Now I am here; I will ensure he understands this henceforth and abide by it."

The President and his men, all hardcore ethnic nationalists, and warriors, had met their match in this simple but forceful old man. They had nothing else to say, and somehow all of them knew the old man had bested them. Oldman Varmie's supreme confidence stems from something else no one in the room knew.

Captain Jimmy Lee and his group of 15 men on November 12, soon after the October 15 election, widely believed to have been won by opposition politician Jackson F Doe, approached the small broadcasting facility from the narrow Redlight end of the Paynesville-Monrovia highway. These men entered Liberia from the Sierra Leonean border and, through a mixture of cunning typographical knowledge and the assistance of collaborators within the army and intelligence services, descended on Monrovia without being intercepted. Once in Monrovia, the group separated, with one group heading for the Executive Mansion, another headed to the BTC Barracks, and the third group moving on to ELBC. The invaders heading to ELBC disembarked from their vehicles at the Joe Bar mini-shopping precinct from the direction of Paynesville Redlight. The few still functioning streetlights cast a faint shadow on them.

Anxious to avoid detection by the small contingent of Army soldiers stationed at the broadcasting facility, the invaders trudged on foot. Now instead of using the darkness to their advantage sneaking upon the soldiers at the entrance of ELBC, Jimmy Lee's men hastily shot up flares illuminating the area. While the flares revealed the position of the defenders, the attackers lost the element of surprise. Wasting no time, the cream of the crop of the Liberian Army opened fire immediately on Lee's men. The attackers were forced to drop to the ground, crawling on their bellies across the road while taking heavy fire.

The small arms fire from the broadcasting facility was augmented by the explosion of shells from the two APCs parked before the entrance of ELBC. Fortunately for the attackers, the shells fired from the APC were not well aimed. They flew harmlessly over the attackers wreaking havoc in the swamp across the market building opposite them. Lee's men replied with automatic rifles, machine guns, and RPG rounds. A fierce firefight was ensured. The attackers made no progress in more than half an hour of sustained fire. The battle quickly reached a stalemate, with the broadcasting station's defenders not attempting to break out of their defensive position. Neither were the defenders receiving any reinforcement from the 72nd Barracks, BTC, or Schiefeillin military bases. The communication system appeared to have been jammed by the defenders of the radio station.

An AFL soldier crouched behind a barrier facing the road and firing attempted using his wireless radio to call for reinforcement. In that instant received a direct hit from a rocket tearing him into smithereens. Using their M203 grenade launchers, the AFL soldiers kept up a small fire and launched grenades at the invaders. Two of the attackers lay wounded, groaning in pain; the attackers had met their match. Journalists inside the facility cowered on the floor in sheer terror.

The attackers at this crucial stage were reinforced by the additional men Quiwonkpa brought in from the Mansion, including some AFL deserters. The pressure on the defenders increased significantly at this point. Realizing their predicament with no reinforcements, the defenders concentrated their firepower towards the main ELWA Junction to Redlight highway attempting to break out. Abandoning their secured position on their armour cars, two defenders dropped to the ground after receiving direct hits. Still shooting, the wounded AFL soldiers shot volleys of small arms fire into the group of armed men approaching them, dropping another two of their attackers dead before they were sent to the great beyond.

The now larger group of attackers split themselves into three groups. Even though the fence protecting the back of the facility was relatively high, some attackers managed to scale the fence. Another group of attackers bypassed the main entrance running and shooting from the direction of a narrow, unpaved road leading to Rehab as a scare tactic to let the defenders know they were outnumbered. There was no hope in continual resistance. Exhausted, running low on ammunition, and disappointed by the lack of reinforcement, the defenders fled.

General Quiwonkpa and his men met no resistance now as they entered through the Iron Gate of the newly built broadcasting house. He ran to the studio guarded by six men to the white broadcasting facility, not bothering to go to the administration building ahead of him to his right. The Eucalyptus trees lining the road to the house swayed under the gentle ocean breeze, oblivious to the violence exploding around it.

"We are freedom fighters of the Patriotic Brigade. Nobody will be hurt, just stay cool and do your job," General Quiwonkpa said.

The new President looked authoritative and dazzling in his olive uniform. Liberia's latest coup maker announced to the shocked but relieved journalists inside the cosy studio that President Samuel K. Doe have been overthrown.

Captain Jimmy Lee produced the priceless transparent blue, black cassette. The frightened journalist on duty could not insert the seditious tape into a large tape deck in the small studio tape recorder. His hands trembled severely. The new President spoke softly, calming the journalist. On his third attempt, the broadcaster managed to insert the seditious tape. The National Anthem then played on the stereo, and then explosive announcement beamed.

The clear, booming voice of Thomas Quiwonkpa, bold and free, no longer a fugitive but an advocate of political violence, announced with all the exigency of a triumphant conquering hero. A hero delivering a message which brought joy to a still-sleeping nation.

"Samuel Doe is a man who has denied the Liberian People their dignity and robbed our nation of its values and significance."

The tape launched into a long diatribe of the litany of abuses perpetuated by the ex-President.

"You shall have your self-worth and dignity restored. I, Brigadier General Thomas Quiwonkpa, Commanding General of the Armed Forces of Liberia, have seized power and have overthrown Samuel Doe's despotic regime. I am now your President until free and fair elections, in which I will not be a candidate, are held within a year. Samuel Doe is in hiding. There is no escape for him."

Then the names of key military commanders were announced, in addition to the heads of security agencies.

"All soldiers are advised to remain in their barracks and take orders from their new commanders. All former government officials, including the SSS Director, Police, NSA Directors, cabinet ministers, and heads of autonomous government agencies, are to report themselves to the nearest Police station for their own safety. Samuel Doe and his cohorts shall stand trial to account for all the things they have stolen from the country. Our revolution is not about revenge or bloodbath; we only aim to give you fellow citizens a government you can truly be proud of."

By the time the first momentous broadcast of the coup ended in the early hours of the morning, few of the intended audience heard it at first. Thomas Quiwonkpa, a man of exceptional good looks, hiding a slant in one of his eyes, wore American-made dark pilot Ray ban sunglasses and was enjoying his finest hours reaching the peak of Mount Everest of redemption. He was viewing the world from its lofty heights, clad in olive forest green uniforms. Attached to the pockets of his uniform shirts and side pockets hanged grenades. The fate of Liberia lay in General Quiwonpka's hands.

The recording announcing the coup was repeatedly broadcast on state radio and Monrovia's two other private stations, which fell to the invaders without a fight.

The new Head of State journeyed from the studio to inspect his men at the refinery. There was no firing at the country's sole petroleum refinery; government troops simply joined the invading coup makers. By this time, dawn began to break upon the land. Within a few hours, Thomas Quiwonkpa's coup had succeeded beyond his dreams. The speed, efficiency, and willingness of soldiers, though expected, still brought immense happiness and vindication to Quiwonkpa.

By six a.m., Quiwonkpa entered the fortress of BTC to rapturous applause, the nation's premier barrack, the seat of the military's political power called the Barclay Training Center. But this barrack was not the strongest.

Resplendent in his uniform, swift and authoritative in his movement, the charismatic new President entered the barrack in a small tactical jeep amidst cheers from troops. The barrack was a multi-tribal institution of soldiers. Soldiers from the new President's tribe were ecstatic. Significantly, though, the new President's appeal when beyond ethnic affiliation, cutting across the ethnic divide. Soldiers who wanted to be soldiers and wanted the military out of politics rejoiced to see the blazing commanding sight of Thomas Quiwonkpa floating to them like sweet heavenly dreams. All the top echelons of the military were now at the General's mercy.

The imposing General, the Chief of Staff, the Defence Minister, Police Director, the Foreign Minister, and even Vice President Harry Moniba now in handcuffs, were dumped on the football field in the middle of the barrack, sitting prostrate at the feet of the man they vilified for so long, pleading for mercy.

Within the few hours of the coup, all of them were now speaking from the other side of their mouths. Adonis Vonleh, one of President Doe's best friends, became one of the most enthusiastic supporters of the coup. Quiwonkpa had no time for them.

The Vice President was made to make a statement which was recorded, calling on all concerned to cooperate with the new government, and accepting the legitimacy of the Patriotic Brigade government. These senior government officials' homes were never invaded nor were they arrested by the invaders. The invaders were far too few to spread themselves thin to do that. It was men like Adolphus Kaykar, who saved them the trouble in another bizarre twist of fortunes, onetime loyal bodyguards in a repeat scenario of 1980, arrested, handcuffed, beatened, and presented their bosses to the new authorities at the BTC.

What strange emotions and intoxicating power can be. Thomas Quiwonkpa was such a busy man he could not take personal charge of these shrivelling men whose previous powerful status evaporated into thin air. Issuing terse instructions, the new President departed the barracks to secure the ELWA Radio Station. By now most of the inhabitants of the capital were aware of the coup but most of the people in the countryside remained ignorant until 7 am when ELWA, a private radio station, broadcast the coupist messages.

Before that, ELWA radio, their only outlet to the capital, only played sombre gospel music. Local and international news broadcast relayed usually broadcast on the station remained silent. The monotony of music devoid of an announcer's voice continued.

Some keen observers in the countryside sensed something unusual happening in the capital city because of this. Most of the people though continued with their daily activities as usual in the morning. Marketers cleaned their tables to set up wares, school children in colorful uniform were on their way to school oblivious to the events in the capital. In the interior with high illiteracy, people did not pay as keen attention to their radio as their urban counterparts.

On his way to the smaller ELWA facility, the new President of Liberia noticed crowds beginning to assemble on the streets in a celebratory mood. Soon a copy of the momentous cassette became inserted into the tape deck at ELWA Studio. The message of the coup now beamed from Voinjama to Harper, from Yekepa to Buchanan. By mid-morning, crowds of civilians and soldiers alike thronged the streets to celebrate. Almost every hamlet in the nation rejoiced. In Grand Gedeh County, the news of the coup was received in silence for the most part while Nimba County, home of the coup maker, rejoiced.

For a momentous and dangerous event as a coup, the guns were silent, the line of demarcation between civilians and soldiers, between invaders and AFL soldiers blurred, the tight discipline of the invaders flushed like urine down a commode. Overwhelmed by their staggering success, discipline built over the years soon faded. Wives of the invaders, relatives and friends besieged their loved ones with kisses, tears, rejoicing, and showing rapturous joy even though many of these long-lost loved ones were still in the delicate act of consolidating their hold on power or performing sentry duties.

The crowds in the streets were just too large to control. Jimmy Lee and his men began to flirt with the civilians, especially the beautiful women who hero worshipped them. Thomas Quiwonkpa returning from ELWA hastened to return to the BTC, but the adoring crowd could not allow his jeep through. Their infectious praises, their enthusiastic presence overwhelmed his vehicle. Such adulation was hard to ignore even though their action impeded his progress. He waved and smiled. Women took off their lappas and placed them on the ground for him to walk on. The crack of communication radio could not be heard over the deafening voices of the celebrating, ululating, and dancing mob of people.

Jimmy Lee and his principal lieutenants, Master Sergeant Rodney Gweh, logistic officer First Lieutenant Fred Knot, and other commanders, crucial for the success of the coup, threw caution to the wind, drinking and dancing in the streets with civilian admirers. The coup makers forgot, unlike the 1980 coup, they staged against a weak civilian government, this coup was against an entrenched military despot. Again, unlike the 1980 coup, this coup was in no way universally popular with all segments of the Liberian population.

Protected by loyal elite soldiers and on a secured line to the Schiefillin Barracks, the invaders failed to cut when they stormed the lower floors of the Executive Mansion.

President Samuel Doe rallied his troops and said, "Men, I am safe and well. Get ready for us to take our country back from these rabid coup makers."

Hearing their commander-in-chief's voice, soldiers who thought the coup had succeeded were galvanized into action. Soldiers from the 1st Infantry Battalion marched northwest to Monrovia and easily took over the ELWA radio station and broadcast their unflinching message of continuity that the coup had failed. President Samuel Doe was still in charge to the shock and horror of many and the ecstatic, rapturous joy of some. Quiwonkpa's coup started to unravel just as quickly as it succeeded, and that's how Adolphus

Kaykar found himself in the bowels of the earth at the dreaded Executive Mansion underground, awaiting execution when the coup failed.

His father, old man Varmie, was steeped in the ways of his ancestors when he learned to his dismay, that his son was locked in the Mansion underground and went to consult the oracle. The old man, a staunched conservative, refused to embrace Christianity. He crawled to the shrine of Worh. This shrine was in a circular hut adorned with raffia palms with no windows or door in the dense jungle. The old man had come to consult the pagan god of destiny to learn the fate of his son. The message from Worh was cold, brutal, and uncompromising.

"Your son will not live. He will die for his crime!"

It was this stern and harsh message that brought old man Varmie to Monrovia to try and alter the words of Worh. And from all indications, his actions worked. Although both the President and Commissioner Tate were extremely annoyed with Adolphus, and they were bloodthirsty for him, they both found themselves drawn to the aura of this enigmatic countryman.

On the second day of his trip to Monrovia, the President freed Adolphus Kaykar and reinstated him in his former position as bodyguard to Commissioner Edwin Tate. Of course, he swore a blood allegiance never to betray his boss ever again.

Old man Varmie was over the moon at the release of his son. He openly said now he could go the way of his ancestors, and he would do so with a smiling face.

Because his son, Adolphus, was free, this ensured his name and bloodline thrived forever, not just as farmers but as government functionaries, the old man boasted.

Mr. Varmie wasted no time in leaving Monrovia, true to his words to the President. When he arrived back in Kaykar Town in Gbi, he was a man on fire, set on meeting his destiny. The very day he arrived, he ordered his two fattest goats to be slaughtered, and a feast was immediately proclaimed. When his friends urged him to rest until the next day for the feast, he was having none of it. He thundered that his feast is held right away.

Soon with his wives, children, grandchildren, and great-grandchildren with loud music, copious drinks, and food flowing, he said goodbye to his family.

His friend Karkay laughed and said, "See what happiness can do. Varmie, instead of saying good night, is now saying goodbye."

Over rounds of cane juice, everyone burst out laughing. Even as he went to bed, Varmie dressed in his finest African robes made up of expensive country cloth threads, smiled even in his sleep. None of those gatherings around had a clue that old man Varmie meant it when he said goodbye. In an ultimate act of self-sacrifice, he offered Worh his life in exchange for his son's life, and he was given 72 hours to fulfill his mission. When his head wife, Quelleh, went to wake him in the morning, he was lifeless and stiff. A strange smile twirled across his lips.

Adolphus Kaykar, old man Varmie's son, served many years as a loyal aide to Commissioner Tate. Even after the long brutal Liberian civil war, he still managed to maintain his powerful position in the Liberia Immigration Service, maintaining his role as one of the commissioners until today.

While historical figures such as President William R. Tolbert, Gabriel Baccus Mathews, Togba Nah Tipoteh, Ellen Johnson Sirleaf, and others are mentioned in this story, they are for contextual and illustration purposes only. This work is a work of fiction that exists only in the writer's mind. A portion of the story first appeared as part of a novel by this writer called, The Fading Flower, Chapter 7, published in 2014 by IUniverse.

Who will tell the President

Liberia was reeling, almost shaken to its core foundation, and the government was teetering on the brink of collapse. Since 1847, the settlers and their descendants have ruled Liberia. For many years this small, isolated country stood as a beacon to the Black race during the time colonialism swept the continent. Europeans were busy carving out pieces of the African pie at the Berlin Conference, with each nation declaring its sphere of influence and control.

This conference was meant to avoid conflict among competing powers in the European land grab. Yet, strangely, the people whose fate was being decided were not part of the conference. Liberia stood as the exception in Africa, defying the logic that the Black race could not govern themselves outside European control and guidance. Haiti and Ethiopia were the other black nations that bulked the trend of European political and economic domination apart from Liberia in the entire world.

Now though, all was not well in paradise. Although the elites in Liberia enjoyed some of the highest standards of living in Africa, the vast majority of the people wallowed in poverty and disease. By the mid-1970s, the efforts of reforming President William R. Tolbert began to yield results. Liberians from the interior, from poor economic backgrounds, were sent to America on government scholarships and began to return to the country. Influenced by the stay and stay in America, these young intellectual firebrands' ways and thoughts differed from the old placid ways of old where people would say, 'yor leave de people thing.' These young intellectuals, primarily men, wanted change and wanted it now. They were Baccus Mathews, Togba Nah Tipoteh, Amos Sawyer, Ellen Johnson Sirleaf, Karn Karlor, and so on. These young radicals, progressives, subversives, or whatever name one may wish to call them, succeeded in raising the political consciousness of Liberians through agitation and activism. Turmoil and uncertainty reigned in Liberia. Conservatives wanted the old way of elite settlers' families controlling everything in Liberia with stability and the grandiose lifestyle based on southern aristocracy in America. Progressives wanted to change and wanted it yesterday. The President was caught between the two opposing forces, almost paralyzed.

Domestic instability in Liberia was a cause for concern in faraway Washington DC, the American capital. Still, the Americans were more concerned about the direction President William Richard Tolbert was taking the country. It was the height of the cold war. President Tolbert had become increasingly non-aligned, opening Liberia up to the Soviet Union, and sided with Egypt in breaking up diplomatic relations with Israel, a nation whose Liberia's vote at the UN helped create. After the poisoning of the US Ambassador in Liberia and the April 14 rice riot, Washington knew it was time for President William R. Tolbert to go.

Miles Spider was a cold warrior to the bone. A man uneasy with peace viewing every peace overture from the Soviet Union as a ruse to gain a tactical advantage in their twilight struggle with the capitalist west. Miles Spider carried his beliefs of good versus evil in the capitalist struggle against communism with missionary zeal. No other evil had befallen mankind than the accursed teachings of Marx and Engels in the form of Godless communism seeking to overwhelm the forces of freedom represented by the capitalist free enterprise system practiced in the United States. An absolutist, Miles believed communism must be nipped in the bud by whatever means possible in any part of the world. Miles would not rest his war, and he was willing to battle in any part of the world where communism reared its ugly head, especially in the dark continue of Africa among newly independent states. Liberia had close historical links to his country; it puzzled him that President Tolbert's government dared become a leading member of a communist front organization like the Nonaligned Movement, giving aid to communists masquerading as freedom fighters in Angola, Mozambique, and other places on the continent. Soon, if the present trend continued, Liberia would fall into the communist sphere of influence, thus enslaving the freedom-loving people of the country.

America, the beacon of freedom, would lose some strategic assets in this country. Though Liberia was geographically a small nation, it possessed an influence far beyond its size. Newly independent states came to her shores to seek advice as Africa's oldest republic. Losing this country to the communist as it was headed under the administration of President Tolbert would be a significant loss of face for Washington. Reared in the austere tradition of the conservative Christian right, Mile's politics and religion were fused together. To prevent Liberia from becoming a socialist nation, American Evangelist, Danny Craven, was brought to Monrovia. Every detail of visitors from the eastern bloc and rogue states heads of government that visited the black republic was crammed in the briefcase of Miles safely stored at his home in northern Virginia since his decision to visit Liberia.

True to form, the cold warrior arrived in the country on a direct Pan Am flight from New York's JFK Airport to Liberia's Roberts International Airport as Evangelist Danny Craven. A team of senior local clergymen was on hand to welcome the distinguished American clergyman. This nation was reeling from the unprecedented civil disturbances of the rice riot of April 14. The youthful opposition leaders spearheading the call for change had been arrested and were being tried for treason. The nation had extended itself after the violence, which shocked the nation and terrified the elite; a somber, reflective mood prevailed. Would Prof. Martins, Baccus Mathews, Amos Sawyer, Adonis Valley, Emory Lomax, and other student leaders imprisoned in the aftermath of the riots be found guilty of treason and hanged as was specified in Liberian law? Could the forces of law and order adhere to the longing for change and introduce radical reforms to improve the dichotomy in society between the haves and have-nots? Or would they react with even more repression due to the threat against their authority by a population longing for change?

These and many other questions plagued the nation in 1980 when Evangelist Danny Craven's plane touched down at the airport. The tall blond-haired Evangelist from North Carolina smiled in the sweltering hot tropical climate. He greeted the distinguished-looking group of clergymen men dressed in the finest African robes and bishopric clothes to welcome him just outside the arrival terminal. Danny looked each clergyman in the eye and flashed a brilliant smile. He took time shaking the hands of the dignified men with thick lips and curly hair, one by one by their names, which he memorized. The raw heat and humidity hit with a bang.

"Welcome to the sweet land of Liberty, Evangelist Danny Craven," Bishop Ted Roland, the tall, dark-skinned bespectacled head of the Episcopal Church of Liberia, announced in his well-modulated baritone voice. "We hope the Lord will use you mightily to save souls in our land."

"Hallelujah, brother Bishop, the Lord does move in mysterious ways, and I know this crusade will bless this wonderful land."

"This way, Sir," the frocked overweight Methodist Bishop wearing long paint robes adorned with a large crucifix pointed, leading the way to a dark tinted-window van waiting. The ignition started, and the engine zoomed to life. Soon the team was headed to Monrovia.

The American Evangelist introduced his team members, singer Al Kane and his backup singers, Evangelist Philip Murphy, and prayer warrior Shiela Kims, both small arm and communication surveillance experts. The drive from the airport to Monrovia was a lovely drive through coastal mangroves, low bush dotted with Palm and Rubber trees, and tall grass dotted here and there. A narrow single-lane highway snaked through lush vegetation dotted with isolated homesteads.

Danny Craven watched the fleeting shadows and relaxed to admire the scenery. But, unfortunately, his attention to the enthralling scenery was constantly distracted by the enthusiastic babble of the ministers rattling on and on. Speaking incessantly about their burning desire to save their countrymen's souls and how the distinguished clergyman's arrival would aid in that process.

"Every generation has a Moses, and I believe, Reverend, God has sent you to be the Moses of our generation to raise disciples for the Lord in our troubled nation."

"Yelp . . . yelp," the Evangelist mumbled without much conviction.

Rev. Adolphus Sayewah, the affable leader of the Baptist Convention, eyes rested on their guest, watching him keenly. Quickly Danny Craven realized he must say something. More was expected of him than just yelp.

"This is true," Shiela Kims chipped in for him. "Our Lord said the harvest is plentiful, but, lo, the laborers are few."

Rev. Sayewah observed the clergyman.

"Our master said, 'go ye into the world and make disciples of all men, baptizing them in the name of the Father, Son, and the Holy Ghost' . . . Mathew 28:19. I hope the Lord will use me to make disciples of all manner of men in this great country," Danny muttered with all sincerity.

The Liberian clergyman smiled. The ice has been broken. Now the conversation became more

Lord-centered. The Evangelist laid a portable bible on his lap, allowing his staff to interact with the clergymen. At the same time, he continued to admire the scenery and concentrated his considerable mental abilities on the elements he needed to contact for his mission. Two boyhood friends hailing from the east had been under Washington's radar for years. The country needed an inexperienced person to take over the reign of power. Lodged in a hotel at Mamba point, Evangelist Danny Craven set up an encrypted communication system that will be used to contact elements in the army without the country's intelligence services, NSA, being able to monitor his calls.

The nation bawled and prayed. The prosecution and defense teams rested their case. They allowed the jury of two women and seven men, all belonging to the establishment, to decide the verdict of the individuals being tried for treason and sedition. Both are grave crimes. The jurors at the impressive Temple of Justice judicial complex spent the first days of their deliberation debating the upcoming party caucus. All the conservative jurors were horrified by the events of April 14 and wanted someone to pay for the destruction wrecked that day. The trial was a sham, and the verdict was a foregone conclusion—guilty as charged. The only point of debate was whether the culprits would face life imprisonment or the death penalty. The pulse of most of the population beat faster and faster on the side of the young idealists. However, people were appalled at the violence of that unforgettable date.

The verdict of the treason trial was tomorrow. Somber religious music dominated the airwaves from ELBC the day before the announcement of the verdict. This trial tore the nation apart like no other trial in the history of this thus far peaceful nation. Everybody knew something had to be done, but nobody knew exactly what to do. In churches, mosques, and fetish shrines around the nation, clergymen and women, imams, and zoes prayed for peace. Even in beer bars, revelers prayed to the force of the universe for peace. It was a time of national upheaval, uncertainty had never been seen before in the sublime, almost perpetually peaceful nation. The stakes were high. To further raise the stakes, the erudite civil President had proclaimed a state of emergency. Security forces were given sweeping powers to do anything necessary for the nation's security.

Inspector Paul Noring, an old-school law enforcement officer, reared in the austere tradition of duty before a complaint, was pleased that the troublemakers were locked behind bars where they rightfully belonged, in a tight corner. His intelligence unit informed him that the strong possibility of widespread social disorder existed if the anarchists were hanged. Perhaps the court could sentence the defendants to death, and then the President could commute the death sentence to a lengthy prison sentence diffusing the situation. A man with his eyes looking for anything out of the ordinary. He scrutinized one of the posters of an American evangelist who entered the country yesterday and posted at the entrance of the police headquarters. *Evangelist! Evangelist! Evangelist!* He kept turning the word in his mind while sipping black coffee at his office. The Evangelist's smiling face and healing crusade sounded altruistic, saving mankind from hellfire. Coming into the country at this time of trouble, something was out of place. The Director kept picking his teeth, thinking, *Danny Craven's coming to the polarized nation to bring healing.* He kept pacing the room, his right fist in his left palm. Inspector Noring flipped on the TV. *Why now? Why now?* He kept muttering to himself.

Even when he drove to his expansive home to Brewerville, situated along the bank of the St. Paul River, he kept mauling over the American evangelist and his healing crusade. He studied the Roberts International Airport passenger list and spent hours poring over every name. Realization, slow and powerful, dawned on him. Then he ran outside to the garage, alarming his wife.

She followed him and said, "Noring, are you going mad? Must it be you alone who must tote this government business on your head?"

Focused on his thoughts, Mr. Noring did not respond to his wife's verbal jabs. He must make haste because if he replies, he will get into a verbal exchange with her, whom he knew would always have the better of the exchange. He fired up his Ford pickup, and as he reversed out of the driveway, he responded, "Monica, I need to see the President immediately. When I come back, I will explain."

"But you are not properly dressed," she replied. "Look at your clothes...."

The last words were lost on the Director as his pickup zoomed out of his yard at high speed, then through the recently built St. Paul Bridge, then towards the Executive Mansion, which was both the home and office of the President. Family links were even more vital than governmental links, and his responsibility was to help care for his auntie's son.

Evangelist Danny Craven could not contain his joy. The long-awaited invitation from the President, for which they rejoiced earlier, was official. CIA agent Miles Spider, aka Evangelist Danny Craven, hastily prepared his kits, including a particularly powerful miniature camera, an ultra-light microphone, a laser gun, and an intoxicating invisible liquid that brought about deep sleep. Satisfied with his packing, Miles examined his false teeth. Again, satisfied, he selected a pristine white monogram shirt and a conservative blue suit for the occasion. The excited agent fumbled through a large time-honored King James Bible, checking his watch for the umpteenth time. Across the street, an unmarked Police vehicle parked unobtrusively observing the scene. Miles Spider drew the curtains of his room apart. A black Mustang that had not been in the vicinity before was parked across the street in front of the Ducor Hotel. He thought and smiled; the *goons tilling him frequently changed cars*. Trained at Langley, he knew how to lose individuals tailing him.

Furthermore, the headquarters of both the NSA and the police were bugged. Miles Spider knew in advance what the security service was planning. Also, Spider knew his driver was an NSA agent, so he just talked about pious religious topics when he was being driven, knowing Momoh. His driver would be debriefed by his bosses. So, the conversation revolved around the atoning sacrifices Jesus Christ made for the sins of mankind, which Momoh fed to his bosses. This invitation from the Liberian President was uplifting. President Tolbert was a preacher and the first black head of the Baptist World Alliance. Psychologists at the agency profiled him and knew the quickest way to get near the President was through religion.

Danny Craven was a Baptist prelate pastoring a small Durham, North Carolina church. Six months before his trip to Liberia, he made a missionary journey to Malawi. The NSA would study his profile and itinerary when he steps foot in Liberia. The word has been going around that the President was loathed when meeting with Americans. Rumors were flying around that the Americans were dissatisfied with President Tolbert's new independent nationalistic trend of wanting a change of government. The first two days Miles spent in Liberia, he visited orphanages and small churches preaching and making modest but significant donations without expressing the desire to meet with the country's political leadership, waiting for the President to initiate contact so he would not seem too anxious to meet the President.

At last intense lobbying by local clergymen, along with the President's own pastoral tendencies, won out, allowing the President to meet the US Evangelist in his official residence. Of course, the President could have agreed to meet him in his hometown of Bensonville, where he entertained his friends and spent the weekends. But that would not serve the purpose of the cold warrior. He wanted a meeting with the President at the Presidential Palace. Now that the invitation had come, he struggled to contain his emotion. The ability to detach oneself from emotion and do the job necessary for God, Country and Family was one of an agent's most prized character traits.

Minutes later, Miles Spider, the veteran agent, accompanied by Rev. Korlubah, the head of the Liberia Missionary and Education Convention (LBMEC), and Bishop Ted Roland, head of the Liberia council of churches (LCC), other senior clergymen, and Rev. Sayewah had transformed into Evangelist Danny Craven. Danny Craven looked distinguished, affable, clean shaven, becoming an epitome of a conservative-friendly man with a burning passion for bringing healing to a nation being torn apart by itself. Cameras flashed and zoomed. Danny Craven smiled as the long sleek limousine conveying him sped through the narrow winding streets of the capital down Broad Street onto Gurley Street and UN Drive. As they journeyed to the Mansion through Lynch Street and Buzzi Quarter, heading to the narrow road gave way to a more spacious boulevard leading to the seat of power.

Danny Craven was absolutely involved in the meticulous study of God's word, evidenced by his deep meditative mood in the black limousine. He mapped out his route from the back of his chauffeur-driven van, reading his bible. The main entrance to the fenced seat of the Presidency was surprisingly very lightly guarded. Vendors selling cigarettes and mints were even trading right at the gate. Furthermore, commercial cars were depositing passengers right in front of the building. A teenager could jump over the low iron fence encircling the Mansion easily. Pedestrians strolled passed the large building from all directions. The limousine carrying the American Evangelist approached the Mansion from the lower direction of the impoverished, densely populated Buzzi Quarter. It branched right, heading straight to the box-sized architecture of the Executive Mansion, which looked dark. Yet the Israeli-built edifice looked elegant. On the left-hand side from the direction of Buzzi Quarter, the rotunda of the Capitol Building glistened in the sun.

Below the arched pathway through which they drove to the main entrance, the clergyman admired the beautiful flower garden of neat, manicured lawns, which added a class to the somewhat austere surrounding of the rigid formality of power. Miles Spider's casual nature possessed an instant aversion to formal rigidity, which had now to endure.

Chaperone by a phalange of bodyguards, the Evangelist, and his Liberian gospel minister companions crowded into an elevator to the sixth floor, the office of the President. Evangelist Danny Craven was received warmly with respect and cordiality. The elevator discharged the guests into an ornate-styled room furnished in an elegant taste. The view and luxury of the room astounded Miles Spider, who imagined the country to be a mosquito-infected backwater. Gold embroidered chairs filled with soft, rich red plumes and pillows occupied the center of the room. Black leather chairs equipped with adorned with hand rests facing a large smooth black mahogany chair. Pictures of the President meeting VIPs from around the world, including a visit to the White House, framed hung on the walls. Large, embroidered drape curtains covered the sliding windows, enhancing the colors of the white mannequin ceilings and silver chandeliers hanging above. The sweet scent of Hibiscus and aloe flowers permeated the Presidential suite with enchanting aloes. Thick wall-to-wall carpets met one's shoe as soon as one exited the polished tiles of the hallway. One could almost see an image of oneself in the veneer wood lining both sides of the Presidential desk, courtesy of the premium quality varnish used on it. Soft electric lights hidden behind chandeliers filled the room, made even more comfortable by the split air-conditioned system.

In a corner to the right of the President's Chair, a large volume of books filled the shelves of a large cupboard-like shelf. Above the shelf, hanged portrays of past Liberian Presidents. Few men possessed the aura of a dignified African statesman as the dark man sitting behind the desk. His face was somber and round; bespectacled, he wore a creamy white suit with dovetailed collars. His shoes matched his clothes. President Tolbert has done away with the long tail three-piece western suits, which have been trademarks of the powers that be in Liberia for so long.

"Welcome, Evangelist Craven; this office has heard much about your good works. The Lord is using you to accomplish much; it is my fervent hope that the Lord will use you to bring healing and reconciliation to our troubled land."

Standing up, the President smiled and extended his hand for a handshake from behind his desk.

"Thanks, President Tolbert, for making time in your busy schedule to grant an audience to my friends and me. I am glad to be in your country and doubly glad to meet you not only as a President of this great nation but also as a clergyman who still preaches in his hometown church."

The President again smiled, shaking the hands of the prominent clergymen who accompanied the American Evangelist.

"Evangelist Danny Craven, you have chosen well using your life to serve your Creator. Exactly what message have you brought us?"

"May we pray," the earnest Evangelist asked.

A request that the President readily agreed to. In a booming voice, Danny Craven announced the prayer was over.

"I have come to bring the children's hearts to their fathers according to Malachi 2:6. To make men study war no more. To let your people know that while politics can divide humankind, Jesus Christ, our Saviour, and Master, can unite. Onesimus, a runaway slave, was told by Paul to return to his master. Even though being a runaway slave was extremely dangerous when the runaway slave was caught. In a letter to receive Onesimus's master, Paul urged him to receive his slave not as a slave but as a brother and co-laborer in the Lord. I have come to President Tolbert. . .," the Evangelist hesitated, speaking slowly with deliberate emphasis to let his words sink in. . . "To proclaim to your nation the message of God's love and the atoning sacrifice of Christ."

The President listened in rap attention as Evangelist Danny Craven espoused the teachings of the good book with infectious enthusiasm. Miles Spider was a natural-born actor endowed with a tempestuous charm that endeared him to all people irrespective of their skin color. He spoke from the script at his hotel supplied by the agency's psychologists, which he rehearsed for so long while his exterior brimmed with enthusiasm; his inner hood squirmed at what he was saying because he did not believe a word of it.

"To whom little is given, little is expected," the President mused. "Sometimes, though for some of us to whom much is given, we wonder whether much is not a curse rather than a blessing. I do not understand how boys I have singled out for their brilliance, provided scholarships for them to study at home and abroad, suddenly turned against my government and me, stirring the people. I know, Evangelist Craven, there are problems, historical problems between the children of the settlers and the children of the tribal people. But past inequalities cannot be reversed within a year. I cannot understand how people nurtured to correct these inequalities against stiff opposition from the old guard could exploit these inequalities against their benefactor to gain political power."

"That is why my message of healing and reconciliation is so important for your nation," Evangelist Danny Craven said.

The President nodded his head in agreement.

Miles Spider wished he had never met this man. This man was treating him with so much respect and being so candid with him, yet it was the downfall of this very man he had come to seek. Evangelist Danny Craven presented the President with a large gold leaf bible ladened with microphones and an invisible powder to make the reader sleep. While handing the President the Bible, he lodged a powerful surveillance camera that could record real-time video and audio of everything happening on the sixth floor.

"Call on me anytime, especially before you leave," the President said.

The President then offered a short prayer before personally escorting the American to the elevator, an honor bestowed on very few visitors. Finally, a sleek limousine drove the American back to his hotel.

In the evening, Danny Craven had to deliver his first major outdoor sermon near the Springs Airfield on Tubman Boulevard. Zero hours was just a few hours away, during which time his contacts, already poised to act, would move against the Executive Mansion around midnight to capture the President. President Tolbert would live the rest of his life in exile. At least this gave the tough agent a little comfort. This man had to leave the Presidency because he was getting too friendly with the eastern bloc nations. The arms and ammunitions were already in the hands of the saboteurs from Nimba, Grand Gedeh, Sinoe, and other interior counties. Key commanders have been separated into those to be bribed, those to be drugged, and those to be eliminated as a last resort.

It was a balmy night in the capital. Earlier, hot, humid Monrovia had a day blessed with unusually calm, fair weather; it was one of those days when the sun did not shine with her blistering intensity, nor did the rain, with her damping wetness, come down. The weather could be described as pleasantly cool, but the heavy relative humidity made it a fair day with a kind of vague efflorescence moodiness attached. This pattern of fair grey weather extended into a breezeless evening. By night cars still clogged the highways leaving the city center for the suburbs. The idle chatter of birds had been absent throughout the day. The President, alone in his office, agonized over the fate of the boys in prison if the judges came out with a guilty verdict.

Danny Craven was also deep in meditation in his hotel room, memorizing his script for the crusade sermon. President Tolbert was kneeling to pray when a weary-looking Inspector Noring burst into his office without an appointment. The President kept him at arm's length, still deep in meditation. Inspector Noring stood impatiently, but protocol demanded that he wait. The drone of the air conditioner made him uncomfortable. The President communed with his God for the next ten minutes, oblivious to the presence of his police chief. Satisfied with his meditation, he rose slowly to his feet.

"What is it this time," he asked in annoyance.

"Mr. President, I have come to warn you never to meet with Danny Craven. He must be deported as an undesirable alien."

"You better be careful about what you say about the Lord's servant otherwise, you may face the wrath of the Almighty."

"Mr. President, we have photos. In fact, there is a witness to prove that the so-called Evangelist has been contacting elements of the army for a coup. Cousin Tolbert, that man is pure trouble."

The President peered over the pictures examining them for a while. He hesitated before speaking. When he spoke, he chose his words carefully.

"Let the man carry out his evangelistic activities tonight. Come with your witness and evidence tomorrow morning. Watch his movements after the crusade. I am too stressed today to investigate such a matter. Contact the Justice and Defence Ministers to be here with you tomorrow morning. Leave me in peace right now."

"President Tolbert ah...."

"I say leave, Cousin Noring, now before I lose my temper and appetite."

"Okay, Sir."

Inspector Noring boarded the elevator with a sinking sensation in his stomach; he had failed to warn the President, his first cousin from the mother's side, sufficiently about Danny Craven's nefarious activities. His evidence, the Director knew, was circumstantial, but his bones told him there was something more sinister about the Evangelist with the beaming smile than meet the eyes.

Miles Spider listened with keen interest to the conversation between the Police Chief and the President. It was imperative that action be taken sooner rather than later. The Evangelist counter-checked his plans to make sure everything was in order. Meanwhile, thousands of Liberians, young and old, thin, and fat, whole and handicapped, sighted and sightless, journeyed to the eastern suburbs to hear the good news of Jesus Christ. The soothing and saving message of God in a scary, uncertain time is to be delivered by Evangelist Danny Craven, whose hope-filled voice had recently saturated the nation's airwaves.

The platform for the occasion in the open air was constructed of planks. White clothes printed with bold letters filled with salvation messages encircled the platform teeming with singers, pastors, instruments, and PA Systems. Large speakers placed in strategy corners ensured that even those outside the perimeters of the crusade venue heard the message. Many people came with deformed children hoping for divine intervention. Bold printing on clothes throughout the crusade venue announced: *JESUS CAN SET YOU FREE!*

Singing and dancing by an enthusiastic crowd reverberated everywhere at the Springfield airstrip. Many hoped for a miracle and divine intervention. Banners announced, *THERE IS HOPE IN CHRIST.* The sheer enthusiasm of the crowd filled the atmosphere with an air of expectation. Local pastors introduced the Evangelist with lavish praise at the end of an hour of intoxicating praise and worship. A sea of humanity of curly hair, thick lips, and gallant features became silent when the Evangelist drew close to the microphone. At that moment, the chain-smoking white saboteur, political missionary, and cold warrior dedicated to nibbling communism and socialism in the bud metamorphosized into a passionate advocate of Christianity. His voice echoed loud and clear, interrupted by frequent cheers from an enthusiastic audience. Cripples were throwing their clutches away because of miraculous healing. Thousands came forward to receive Christ, while many others came forward to renew their commitment to God. Trained counselors rushed to talk to them about their salvation. At that moment, a buzz sounded in the microphone hidden in Miles Spider's ears—the dogs of war were moving on the President. He heaved. How had he wanted to take a stiff drink: but how could he now?

Soon after the crusade, Evangelist Danny Craven caught the last Pam Am flight out of Liberia when he received the coded words that the eagle had landed.

Shiela Kims stayed behind to coordinate with the non-commission officers soon to be in charge.

Liberia awoke to unprecedented, startling, and revolutionary news shaking the foundation upon which the nation-state rested. The news swept the foundation of the old order, lock, stock, and barrel. It was joyous, spontaneous, tumultuous, and highly traumatic simultaneously. It brought the unknown, the weak, and hitherto powerless into the very den of power. Bringing the erstwhile rich and powerful into sudden subjugation, ridicule, and powerlessness never seen in the land. This startling change was poignant by its dramatic manifestation and brute force. Listeners to early morning shows on the airways were surprised, stunned, and stupefied by the announcement on the radio. Strange and dreamlike, it seemed as if occurring in some distant land. The labored, unrefined, heavily accented voice with a peculiar twang, unrehearsed and unsophisticated, belonging to one unpractised in the diction of broadcasting, echoed in listeners' ears. But the voice carried a certain tone of ruthlessness and frenzied command bordering on morbid hysteria was time to act.

President Tolbert had been killed in his own bed, and a new group of henchmen called the People's Redemption Council was in charge of Liberia. While it saddened Miles that the former President died gruesomely, he was glad his maddening flirtation with the nations of the eastern bloc had suddenly come to an end.

Next week he would be headed to Nicaragua to arrange arms drop-off by the agency to Contra guerrillas fighting the left-wing Sandinistas.

This story is set in 1990 in Vahn Town, a small town in Lower Nimba, during the early days of the Liberian war that will make you laugh.

It all ends well

The village of Vahn Town is situated a little more than a dozen kilometers south of Tappeta. The neighborhood comprised some corrugated zinc-roofed buildings and dirt brick with palm-thatched structures. In the community, old lady Wready had earned the reputation of being a tough, sassy, and feisty old woman. Even young kids there knew to avoid her; her razor-sharp tongue knew no bounds nor feared any authority.

It was the beginning of a fratricidal civil war in Liberia, and the atmosphere was thick with fear and uncertainty. One afternoon the men in green, as was the habit in the climate of fear and uncertainty, had gone on patrol from their garrison in Tappeta. The patrols by government soldiers in these parts were basically to steal livestock. Butuo and Karnplay, where the war was reported to be raging, were far from Tappeta. Who dares question the men with guns in green? They were all men!

Everyone looked over their shoulders and watched every word uttered in the presence of government officials now. While life continued almost normal in Monrovia, here in Nimba County, a fratricidal conflict raged away from the eyes of the international community and journalists. Those border towns of Butuo and Karnplay were said to have been captured by rebels. But why would the insurgents' advance southwards to capture Tappeta instead of going to Ganta and Gbarnga on their way to Monrovia to remove President Samuel Doe from power?

That did not make sense. Therefore, the AFL soldiers were not unduly worried. They pilfered livestock and carried out harassment targeted primarily at young men. Knowing that as soon as villagers hear the distinct sounds of their American-made military vehicle, everyone in sight disappeared into the surrounding bushes as far as their legs can carry them. The soldiers quickly learned that empty towns meant houses waiting to be looted at will. But somehow, empty towns contributed to a sense of isolation and ostracization from the community. Almost all the government soldiers hailed from other parts of Liberia and were non-local. Instead of driving their jeep straight into the villages to alert villagers to run before they arrived in the town, the soldiers adopted a new tactic.

Approaching a town or village, the soldiers would stop and park their cars a kilometer or two from the town and then advance on foot to catch the villagers unaware. It was essential to see the villagers in town. AFL soldiers did not want to undergo the indignity of running after a goat, chicken, sheep, or pig and toting the loot to their cars. It was much easier, convenient, and more dignified for local boys to put the 'captured' livestock into their jeep.

On this day, the strategy worked brilliantly in Vahn Town. Parking their vehicle between Vahn Town and Segbeah Town, the group of 15 soldiers trekked on foot to deal a decisive blow to insurgents through the consumption of hot goat pepper soup from stolen meat. That evening the men in green stumbled upon a group of young men standing and talking in low excited voices while grouped together listening to a single transistor radio. The women and children spent their days in the security of their farms away from the town, protected by the dense jungle, only returning to sleep in the town at night. The young men shaking in fright, frequently huddled around the town near the Drab public elementary school to hear the latest gossip and exchange information about politics and purported rebel advances but were always anxious to flee at the sound of moving vehicles.

The surprised group of young men found to their horror staring straight into the barrels of automatic rifles. One Foot Devil, the nom de guerre of one of the AFL's feared sergeants, shouted an obscenity.

"Halt! Any of you seen rebels around here?"

"No, Sir," a young man in his late twenties who seemed to be the group's leader responded.

One Foot Devil apprised him with pure contempt written across his face.

"Maybe you are the rebels!"

"No, officer, please, we are not. We love the government!"

"Love the government, my foot, damn Gio rebels!"

"Ok, show you love the government. Each of you must catch one chicken and a goat and take them to our car! And soldiers!"

"Yes, Sir!" his men responded.

"If any of these rebel sympathizers attempt to run to the bush, shoot him dead because he is a rebel!"

"Sir," his men shouted in unison.

The group of young men did not need to be told what to do, and so the chase began. The soldiers followed somewhat leisurely as the young men rounded goats and chickens.

Somehow, old lady Wready had been delayed going to the farm that day. From the corner of her eyes, she saw something she could not believe. Tiatune's son, Sarday, was running behind her biggest and most prized rooster, no doubt to catch it. She had not negotiated to sell the rooster to anyone or attempt to sell it.

"You good for nothing, Sarday. I didn't know you have turned into a rogue. If you dare lay hands on my rooster. I will make sure you rot in jail! I will sue you and your parents, who are poor like church house rats! And I will make sure you pay double for my rooster! Nonsense!

Just then, fuming with righteous indignation, old lady Wready lifted her head, looking right into the barrel of the soldier's gun. She broke into a broad smile.

"My son, you are catching the rooster for the officer; why you didn't tell me? Catch my rooster and the other one behind it; that big one for the officer!"

She bit her lips hard when Sarday grabbed her rooster. He tied the legs and handed the rooster to One Foot Devil with old lady Wready giving an approving look. As soon as the boy and the soldiers went further down to the Kokweah's residence, old lady Wready looked around and dashed into the bush, running to her farm. It was rumored that Wready never set foot in Vahn Town again until her burial.

1980 Monrovia, in the aftermath of the overthrown of the civilian government of President William R. Tolbert, is a chaotic time in Liberia. Renegade soldiers ran amok, preying on the formerly rich and powerful brought down by the coup. One of these bands of renegade soldiers picked up Tom in his home that night, whisking him to an unknown destination.

Dance of the fathers

The streets of Monrovia exploded into rapturous joy in a way the tiny West African nation had never seen in its history. From Dualla Market to Paynesville, Rally Time Market to Jorkpen Town market to Joe Bar, the crowd thronged the streets, dancing with extreme zest, hugging strangers, and cheering as patriotic songs played on state radio. Liberians have gone to bed weary and sad. They were now awoken to the unprecedented news that oppression under an Americo-Liberian hegemony had been swept into the dustbin of History.

An uncompromising group of young soldiers, through a stunning act of violence and aggression, burst into the president's office, killing him, and announcing the overthrown of the old True Whig Party government replacing it with a military junta which they named the People Redemption Council. The men of the junta whose unrefined voices filled the airways nevertheless brought Liberians to the streets in Voinjama, Harper, Sanniquellie, Robertsport, and everywhere although they were virtually unknown. Who was Samuel Kanyon Doe? Thomas Quiwonkpa? Wei Sehn or Nelson Toe?

Who cared?

Could they have come from Mars or Pluto as long as the soldiers brought liberation to the majority of the people of Liberia?

But not everyone was thrilled by the prospects of young semi-literate soldiers bursting onto the national scene and executing former government officials on public beaches, much to the delight of their young supporters bailing for blood on the streets.

Tom Sonkarlay was a man who worked extremely hard through the ranks, from a schoolboy in a thatched one-room school building in a nameless village to a Minister responsible for curriculum development in Liberia. Then the men with guns took over, and life changed for Tom. Imprisoned and shackled in a military prison, Tom awaited execution. Even though he was a civilian, the court and judge trying him and his colleagues was a military one that brought down guilty verdicts in closed sessions where no independent observer, the press, or ordinary person was allowed to witness the proceedings. Day and night, Tom prayed for God to give him a second chance. In his bargain with God, he promised to live a more religious life if God spared him from the executioner's bullets. Tom pledged to God to be more faithful, to give up his love of booze, and give more to the poor.

And to Tom's surprise, God heard him, giving him a second chance. One morning it happened; when Tom and other prisoners were brought out to exercise in the sandy beachside barracks of the Barclay Training Centre, Liberia's most extensive military barracks.

Forced to play football on the beach as a form of exercise, Harrison Pennue, a maverick member of the junta, took one look at Tom, and it was over. Harrison was a cousin of the new head of the junta. Rumour had it he was the one who stabbed the former president, William Tolbert, in his bed, killing him. A small man of unpredictable temper, many feared and respected him. That day, Pennue happened to be at the barracks visiting his men.

"Who is that man," he shouted, looking, and pointing in Tom's direction. "Bring him to me!"

Two soldiers immediately grabbed Tom and shoved him forward. Tom squeezed his knees together and put his hand over his privates as if he wanted to pee. A broad smile broke across Pennue's dark, handsome face.

"What is your name?" Pennue asked.

"Tom Sonkarlay."

"I don't care what this man did," Pennue said. "I like him. He reminds me of my father. He will be my father from today. Mr. Sonkarlay, you are a free man. Whoever asks, say I, Colonel Harrison Pennue, free you. Get your belongings. I'm taking you to your house right now!"

And just like that, Tom Sonkarlay became free from death row and was a free man. It was extraordinary because the following morning, all his fellow inmates were executed. For an unknown reason, Pennue had taken a liking to him.

Tom was happy to be out of prison and spending time with his family. Then one night, it seemed like something sinister hung in the air. A group of five young soldiers carrying M-16s and Israeli-made UZI submachine guns made their way to Tom's house. They all looked under twenty-five. Tom sat with them in his living room, waiting to hear the reason for their visit and stirring at him in a very strange.

"Mr. Tom Sonkarlay," one of the men said. "The Head of State, Samuel K. Doe, wants to see you effective immediately . . . without delay."

"The Head of State wants to see me tonight? Why?"

"Sir, we are only obeying orders. We have no idea why the Head of State wants to see you. It could be an appointment or consultation . . . whatever it is. Could you hurry? We have orders to obey."

Why would the Head of the state want to see me in the middle of the night? Tom thought. "Can I go tomorrow," he asked. "I will make sure I obey the president's request first thing in the morning."

"Sir, you are wasting our time," the same soldier said. "This is an order, do not make us force you. Besides, there are other people in the house, including children."

It seemed an ominous warning—Go with us or put your family, including kids, in danger.

"Let me put on some clothes," Tom requested.

With a sinking feeling of impending doom in his stomach, Tom quickly put on a nice shirt and a pair of monogram trousers to go with the men whose demeanor showed they would not be patient for too long.

Suddenly, there was a knock at the door, and Africanus, Tom's older sister's son, walked in. He, too, was a soldier, albeit serving in a different role, it seems, from the men waiting in his uncle's living room. Africanus was home practicing a new song he had composed for the army band.

"I felt a strong desire to come and see you, Uncle," Africanus said to Tom.

He noticed Tom's wife and two daughters had tears in their eyes.

"Thanks for coming, Nephew," Tom said. "But the Head of State just sent for me . . . I must leave with Lt Peter Gayflor."

Dressed in civilian clothes and unarmed, Africanus looked at the men, closely examining their faces. None of the men looked familiar to him except the quiet sergeant with steely brown eyes standing near the door. Besides that, there was nothing much he could do. His offer to go with his uncle and the soldiers was flatly rejected.

The Sonkarlay family watched Tom go, sandwiched between two soldiers. A thousand thoughts crossed his mind as they drove by houses and trees, thinking it might be his last time here. The small Mazda meandered its way through the narrow, unpaved road in Gardnerville unto the Somalia Drive highway linking Freeport to the commercial district of Redlight.

The Mazda turned on the main paved road towards Freeport, heading to town. Tom felt a little relief; the car was driving toward town, no doubt leading to the barracks. This meant the soldiers were telling the truth. Everyone in the car was a soldier, even the driver and the passenger in the front seat.

Then to Tom's dismay, when they got to the Freeport junction, the car veered right. That road led to Dualla or Caldwell, far away from the direction of the president's location or the junta. Again, a thousand thoughts railroad through his mind. A sense of déjà vu filled Tom, who sat quietly as they drove further away from the city into the isolated suburbs. As soon as the taxi crossed the St. Paul bridge, the car stopped and parked a little way from the road.

"Wait here for us," one soldier said to Tom as they all got out of the car.

Tom could not see where they had disappeared, but they were not far. He could hear them chatting in audible whispers from a short distance.

"Guys, we have to take the man back to his family," someone said.

"What the hell are you saying?" asked another. "We must carry out our original plan. Let us kill this man and make sure that no one ever finds his body."

"Yes . . . yes," the other soldiers mused in agreement.

"Right, you all can say that," the soldier who wanted them to take Tom back said. "You do not know Africanus, his nephew, who came in just as we were about to leave the house. He knows me from BTC. If Tom is not seen, his nephew will tell Harrison Pennue that his favorite Papay was last seen alive in our company. Do you know what that means?" he asked and answered, "Firing squad for us."

"Say for you, but not for me," one of the soldiers said. "African or whatever you call him knows you and not me."

"And you think I'm a fool because I'm putting more thoughts into this?"

No one answered.

"As soon as they come for me, I will start singing your names like a bird," he continued.

In the main time, Tom thinks about dashing for freedom, but the men are within view of the car and could see and shoot him if he tried to escape.

Their argument grew fainter and fainter until he could no longer hear them. Then, soon the soldiers returned to the car and got in, sandwiching him again. The driver started the engine and took off, this time driving northward toward the direction of

Browerville. Tom Sonkarlay knew he was done for. Maybe he should have tried to escape.

The driver suddenly made a U-turn, headed toward the direction of Dualla, and stopped abruptly.

"Papay," he said, showing his opened palm over his seat in Tom's face. "Pay for our petrol . . . we are taking you back home."

"I thought we were going to see Head of State Samuel Doe?" Tom asked.

"Mr. Tom," he said, "God has given you a longer life. Just pay for our petrol."

Tom realized it was no time for blustering. He took out a ten-dollar bill and put it in the man's hand. The driver took the money, directed his attention to the road, and drove slowly as they headed back to Gardnerville.

For ten years, Tom Sonkarlay knew God had given him a second chance. What made his nephew, who seldom visited him—because he was a relic, a bourgeoisie of the old order, come to see him at night on the spur of the moment? The soldiers change their minds. And it was ten glorious years spared to watch his children grow and do things that family do together.

Ten years later, in 1990, when Tom Sonkarlay heard that rebels had invaded Liberia, he could not shake those feelings of trepidation and doom. I heard him tell his son, Tom Sonkarlay Jr., that if they were together and something happened, his son should try and escape and leave him. Up to today, I still wonder whether Tom was two times lucky and survived the fratricide in Liberia, or did his fear of impending doom come true?

Author

Mr. Nemen M. Kpahn is an oral storyteller in the West African griot tradition of vivid storytelling. A writer and author of this new collection of short stories: Dance of My Father and other stories, telling enthralling stories is his passion.

From a young age, Kpahn's deep and abiding interest in the written word made him devour most of the novels in Heinemann's famous African Writers Series, starting with People of the City, a novel by Nigerian writer Cyprian Ekwensi. That fascination with words and their usage led him to study and obtain a Master of Communication degree from

Griffith University and a Master of Research degree from the University of Southern Queensland.

Kpahn uses a unique descriptive writing style to bring to life characters from Liberia's dance with death during the ruinous civil wars of the 1990s. His characters spring to life from the pages of his writings in A Naked Lie and other stories, The Fading Flower, and two children's books: Little Brave Lydia and Drama on Pipeline Road. Telling stories about ordinary people facing extraordinary obstacles with courage and humor reminds readers not to forget Liberia's history.

Mr. Kpahn has traveled extensively to the United States, India, Dubai, Qatar, and Morocco, and he is eager to see and discover new things and opportunities. He lives in sunny Brisbane, a sub-tropical city with warm summers and mild winters in Queensland, Australia. He spends his spare time reading and exploring the quirkiness and exhilarating and, at times, tragic Australian outback.

Books by Nemen M. Kpahn
Find these books at all book stores and online:

The Fading Flower

A Naked Lie and
Other Stories

Drama on Pipe Line
Road

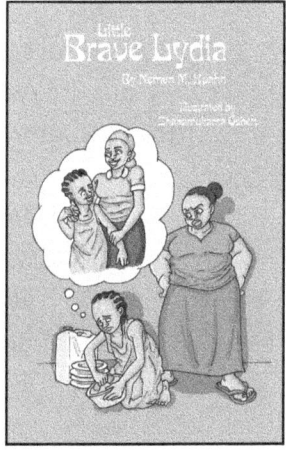

Little Brave Lydia

Village Tales Publishing provides traditional publishing services and turnkey services to individuals that seek to successfully self-publish and promote their books. We handle all aspects of publishing; editing, cover design, production, marketing and order fulfillment.

Please visit our websites:
www.villagetalespublishing.com
www.villagetalescreatives.com

Join our mailing list for updates on new releases, deals, bonus content, and other great books from Village Tales Publishing.

Email Us:
villagetalespub@gmail.com
info@villagetalespublishing.com
****

Like Us on Facebook
www.facebook.com/villagetalespublishing
Follow Us
@villagetalespu